SEVEN GHOSTLY SPINS

—a brush with the supernatural

Patricia Bossano

Ft. Kelsey E. Gerard

Seven Ghostly Spins–a Brush with the supernatural

This book includes the author's interpretation of personal experiences and variations of true local legends and it is ultimately a work of fiction. Names, characters, businesses, places and incidents are either used fictitiously or are the product of the author's imagination.

Cover design and art by Christina Wilson.

Published in the United States by WaterBearer Press
PO Box 302078
Escondido, CA 92030
www.waterbearerpress.com

ISBN: 978-1-7325093-0-6 (hc)
ISBN: 978-1-7325093-1-3 (sc)
ISBN: 978-1-7325093-2-0 (e)
ISBN: 978-0-9994346-9-7 (sc arc)

BISAC: Adult Fiction, General: Action & Adventure | Anthologies | Fantasy | Paranormal | Ghost | Horror | Occult & Supernatural | Short Stories | Thrillers | Supernatural

Library of Congress Control Number: 2018909827

WaterBearer Press Edition: November 2018

Al correo de las brujas y las brujitas,
…may we live on and prosper.

CONTENTS

ACKNOWLEDGMENTS

To formally dispel all the misleading talk about "writing being a lonely business" or "writers being lone wolves," I hereby incorporate *you* into my tribe and include you in my upcoming award acceptance speech because, as with all my other books, I could not have done this without *you*!

My heartfelt gratitude to the courageous individuals who agreed to beta-read *Seven Ghostly Spins*—I know it is a tough job and I couldn't have found a better group for the task. It takes a special someone to take time from their busy schedule to peruse unedited manuscripts and make sense out of them, so thank you: Paul, Carmen, Outi, Kelsey, Kirk, Sherry, Deborah, Tiffany, Literary Titan, you are top-shelf in my opinion and I cannot thank you enough for your candid insight and thorough critique! When you read the final version, I hope you'll see your influence reflected in the pages.

The core of my tribe is made up of family and friends without whose unconditional support, encouragement, supernatural artistry, and generous sponsorship I wouldn't get anything written. Thank you for continuing to believe in me; Blanca, Kelsey and Remy, Paul, Carmen, Alex, Martín, Nicole and Julio, Silvia, John, Linda and Camila, all my aunts, uncles and cousins all over the continent. And a grateful shout-out too, to the latest additions to my team: Simone & Co., Christina Wilson, Isabelle Maynard, Colin Graham Publishing Group, you rock!

A most radiant thank you to: Luis, María, Esteban, Renee, Carolyn, and all my other departed dears for your continued trans-dimensional guidance in my journey.

And to you, the reader, I am overwhelmed with gratitude that you picked up this book!
I hope you will enjoy reading this compilation of flights of fancy inspired by Southern California landscapes, local legends from Northern Utah, and mind-bending experiences from my childhood home in Ecuador.

Happy Reading!

ALIS⊕N

Patricia Bossano

No self-respecting theater House is without its ghost

May 1924

"Okay, my little Nut, let's hear it," Papa says.

I grin and snuggle into my pillow. "Now I lay me down to sleep, I pray the Lord my soul to keep. If I shall die before I wake, I pray the Lord my soul to take. Amen."

"Amen," he echoes and kisses my forehead before turning off the light.

"Sweet dreams," Mamma says as she places a folded piece of cardboard over my nightlight. It's covered with holes; Papa poked them on it so my ceiling looks like it's filled with stars. "Nut will watch over you too," she whispers and kisses me goodnight.

I smile looking at my starry ceiling, thinking about my papa's work—for months he's been telling us all about it.

My papa is a stonemason and he was hired by the two Mr. Peerys to build the magical movie palace. He says there is only one other building like it in the whole United States. That is because it has a sky ceiling—an "at-mos-phe-ric dome" Papa calls it. He says the indoor sky will change from morning to night, and it will even have clouds! And Mamma, who is a schoolteacher, has been explaining to my brother and me about the Egyptian legends. She's told us all about the tomb of King Tut that somebody found, just a couple of years ago in Egypt, and since then, the whole country's been in a fever—even us—about mummies, treasures, and gods and goddesses.

My favorite legend is the one about Nut. She is the Egyptian goddess of the sky. In Mamma's book the painting of Nut shows her protecting the whole world with her body; she is opened like an umbrella over us, and her bent back is the sky full of stars—yes, she is my favorite.

I close my eyes and see myself drifting through the night sky, dreaming that I can touch those stars.

* * * *

"Alison, baby girl, are you ready?" Mamma calls.

"Almost," I say, buckling my shoes and tying a ribbon like a headband knotted at the back of my neck—that will have to do until my hair is long enough to wear in a ponytail; for now, though, it barely reaches my shoulders.

I race out of my room to the kitchen. Mamma's got the sandwiches ready; she fixed them with the roasted chicken left over from last night's dinner. She looks me up and down and smiles. "Don't forget the cookies."

I pull out the two biggest from the jar (I baked them this morning) and wrap them in a napkin, frowning at the chocolate chips already staining the white cloth—I'll just have to scrub it later.

I can't wait to see what the Egyptian Movie Palace looks like inside; Papa promised I could go in today, so I'm bringing us lunch and we'll have us a scaffolding picnic.

Since we live only a block away, Mamma is letting me walk over there.

"Now you be careful crossing the street," she says.

"Yes, Mamma." I give her a kiss and I'm out the door, clutching the lunch basket and a bottle filled with juice.

"And be back by two." She waves from the front door.

"Yes, ma'am," I call back, turning to look at her one last time. She looks so pretty in her flowered dress and white apron. She smiles and blows me a kiss.

Skipping on the sidewalk down 25th Street, I don't even notice the heat and the sunshine—they're nothing to me because all I can think of is the dark, cool inside of the theater and the ceiling filled with twinkling stars, in the middle of the day!

Looking both ways before crossing Washington Boulevard, I hurry the rest of the way to the movie palace.

As I go by the box office with my basket and juice, I see lots of men working in a cloud of fine dust that makes me want to cough. A couple of construction workers tip their hats at me. I nod politely but dash past them.

Papa said to go to the right of the auditorium, which, just like he said, looks like the pictures in Mamma's book of the open court of an Egyptian temple!

It's dark. There are only a few lights, mainly on the scaffoldings where men are working. Something happens to my ears in there, like someone stuffed cotton balls in them, but then I remember what Papa said about acoustics and I settle down.

Papa is on the scaffolding along the wall, farthest from the stage. I stand there for a few minutes, watching him. He is concentrating hard, with his trowel and mortar handy.

"Hey, sweetie, aren't you Joe's little girl?"

The deep voice makes me jump—had the bottle not been capped, orange juice would have sloshed everywhere. "Yes, sir."

"Didn't mean to startle you," he says kindly and walks me over to the foot of the scaffolding.

"Hey, Joe! A young lady is here to see you."

"Thank you," I murmur.

"Don't mention it," he says with a wink.

"My little Nut! You're here already?" Papa calls down, leaning over the safety bar, and I wave up at him.

He lowers a bucket he has tied to the end of a rope. "Put our lunch in there, and then come up the ladder—I'm on the third floor," he kids.

I giggle nervously as I place the basket and the bottle inside the bucket. He starts pulling it up as I begin climbing the ladder. The scaffold wobbles but I tell myself, only two floors to go.

Papa helps me to my feet and steadies me as I look around, feeling a little dizzy—we're so close to the dome! Papa has pushed his tools to the edge of the boards and cleared the middle of his work surface for our picnic. He sits in the center and pats the spot next to him for me.

He chatters away while I eat slowly, staring wide-eyed at everything: the ceiling, the wet mortar drying next to me, the pink plaster on the wall across from us, the stage, which seems a loooong way down from where we are. And when I look behind me, we are at eye level with the private boxes. I get lost in thoughts of how wonderful it would be to see a show from inside one of those boxes!

"'Wanderer of the Wasteland,'" Papa says, like he was reading my mind. "That's the feature they'll play on opening night only two months from now—it's a silent movie, so the Wurlitzer pipe organ will do the accompaniment," he explains.

"I would much rather see a play," I tell him, imagining real people, acting and singing on the stage, and us, sitting in a private box.

When we finish our cookies, Papa smiles and tells me he has a surprise.

"Lay down right here," he says, setting aside the basket and the empty bottle.

Just like he asked, I stretch out on the boards and stare at the ceiling, waiting. I'm so excited! Papa's surprises are always good!

When he finishes making signals to someone below, Papa lies down beside me.

"Wait till you see this," he says, snuffing his work light and jutting his chin toward the ceiling.

"Oh, Papa!" I gasp, and it comes out with a little bit of a sobbing sound.

The blue dome begins to light up at one end, like morning is coming, while at the other end it's midnight blue, with lots of twinkling stars. Pretty soon, wispy clouds begin to move through as if blown by a breeze. I want to cry, it's so beautiful!

Papa squeezes my hand and I hold tight to his. I want to tell him how much I love this surprise, but nothing comes out—I just keep staring.

"How does the Egyptian prayer go?" he whispers, and I have to clear my throat, or else my voice will shake with all the things I'm feeling. As soon as I'm steady enough, I begin repeating what Mamma had read to me.

"'O my Mother Nut, stretch yourself over me, that I may be placed among the im-pe-rish-able stars which are in you, and that I may not die.'"

"But if either of us does," Papa says, "Nut would take us to her star-filled sky and revive us with food and wine."

"Do you think maybe she would give me milk instead of wine?"

Papa chuckles and I grin, though a tear rolls down the side of my face because I'm so choked up. I wipe it off quickly and ask him another question, trying to make light of my feelings. "How do you think it would be to live here all the time?"

"Oh… I don't know about living here as if it were home. How about just sleeping here, every now and then? Like we're camping in the Sahara Desert," Papa replies seriously. I know he doesn't want to make me feel childish. He squeezes my hand one more time and turns to look at me.

When I look at him, he winks, and I decide it would be *okay* to camp here, although I would much rather *live* here.

"It's a magical place, Papa," I say, turning my head to stare at the indoor sky again. "Papa, do you think the sky really is the goddess Nut, bent over us like in Mamma's book?"

"It's possible—the Egyptians sure believed it," he says reassuringly.

In my head and in my heart, I'm convinced it's true.

"Well, little girl, it's about one-thirty now."

"Yes, sir, and I told Mamma I would be back by two."

"Then we'd better get you down."

Papa gets up and loads the picnic things in the bucket. The scaffolding sways a little with his movements and for a second, I feel like I'm on a raft floating on a river, maybe the Nile.

Papa's tools are still at the edge of the work surface, so I go put them back in their spot, closest to the wall, where he'll be using them. That's when it happened.

It's what Mamma would call a head rush because, I guess, I stood up too fast. Everything turns gray and sparkly as I bend over the tools, and when I try to straighten up, my head hits the guardrail and my body falls forward. I try to grab on to something but there's nothing.

"The third floor," Papa had said, and a rush of hot and cold goes through me when I realize the floor is a long way down.

I don't even have time to imagine the pain I'll feel when I hit the concrete below.

I hear a hollow sound, sort of like that watermelon made when my brother dropped it on the driveway, and then I know it's my head that just made that sound. But I can't feel anything—well, maybe just the cool cement under me.

I open my eyes—there is the starlit sky. There are loud voices all around and Papa sounds like he's growling as he comes down the ladder.

"Don't move!" I think that's what he says, his voice sounds so different, angry or maybe full of fear.

"I'm sorry," I want to say, but I can't, so I lie still, like he told me. If he's angry, I wonder if he'll shake me?

But when he kneels beside me, he doesn't do that, he seems afraid to even touch me.

Wishing he could hear my voice inside my head, I think really hard: "Papa—I'm sorry—I got dizzy…" My eyes cloud with tears. He's crying now. I want to get up but can't move. "Papa—"

He lifts my hand to his lips and kisses it. "Alison, my little Nut…"

More men tower over me; they're all shaking their heads gloomily. The lights are on now, and the stars are gone, but they haven't turned off the clouds—they race so fast across the sky, they make me feel sick.

Papa's eyes say things look bad for me—I won't make it home by two like I told Mamma. I look at the sky and I feel like I'm getting closer to it. The cement doesn't feel so cold, maybe because it's not there anymore, or I'm not on it anymore.

I guess someone's working the lights again. The clouds slow down, and everything is like fire on one side of the ceiling: sunset. And then, there's midnight blue stretching out forever on the other side.

There are so many stars! I could reach out and touch them, if only I could move. For one sleepy moment, I believe I'm back in my room, waiting until tomorrow, when I get to go to the magical movie palace.

"I love you, baby girl, my Alison, my little Nut!" Papa cries, and I think it's strange that I hear Mamma's voice with his; is she here? Maybe I really am in my room, and I just finished saying my prayers…

Then, there's another voice, a breezy one I don't recognize, and she says, "I am Nut, I am here to enfold and protect you from all things evil."

The stars are all around me now. I close my eyes and I float for a while, not in my room but in a dream. I think I should go home but I don't know how. I'm not worried though.

* * * *

When I open my eyes again, the scaffoldings are gone, and the auditorium is full of people. They're sitting on rows and rows of chairs. The air is thick with perfumed smoke. There is music coming from the organ, and a silent movie is playing on the screen.

It's opening night—how time flew!

And I never made it back home…

There are people sitting in the fancy private boxes and below them too. There's a lady wearing a flowered dress; she looks like Mamma! I race over to see her up close, but it isn't her. The stars in the sky ceiling seem to dim with my disappointment, but they light right up again when I think I see Papa and my brother!

It's not them either—I should've known they wouldn't come without Mamma.

Maybe they'll all come for the next show. Of course they will, and I will be waiting for them!

I see a row of chairs right on the spot where I fell, and there is an empty seat. I sit next to a woman who doesn't notice me, and I stare amazed at the screen. Music fills me up.

I *am* home.

I sincerely hope you enjoyed reading this ghostly spin.

The inspiration to flesh out Alison's story came to me during a private tour of Peery's Egyptian Theater. The manager at the time did a wonderful job of showcasing the historic movie palace for me. I saw the place where Alison fell, I sat on her favorite chair—dozens of people have seen her there. I went into the bathrooms where she entertains herself turning the lights on and off, or just letting the water run—per the chuckling janitor who shared his experiences with me.

Because of her innocence and sweet demeanor, Alison occupies a special place in my heart. I hope I've done right by her and that you, henceforth, let her tag along—in your imagination.

* * * *

Factual tidbit about *Alison*:

Peery's Egyptian Theater, Ogden's historic movie palace, is located on Washington Boulevard, between 24th and 25th Streets.

Legend has it that during its construction in 1924, a 12-year-old girl named Alison brought lunch for her father and at some point during her visit she died in a fall, either from scaffolding or from a balcony.

The friendly ghost of Alison, described as having shoulder-length hair, reportedly haunts the boxes in the rear of the theater, though there have also been sightings of her playing a piano, turning lights on and off, and occasionally sitting next to a lucky patron in the audience.

BY THE IRON GATE

Patricia Bossano

When isolated from the bustle of civilization, the mind slips unfettered. Especially a child's.

By the Iron Gate is a flight of fancy, triggered by a *real* nightmare and a *real* walk in the moonlight.

1917

The gardener with the soft brown eyes and the callused hands offered her a cluster of alfalfa flowers that morning. When she took them, she sentenced herself to purposely recall the incident from then on, over and over, just to relive the exotic sensations his gesture had unleashed.

* * * *

She sat on the lip of the square pond, enjoying the warm sunshine. Even through her stockinged feet, encased in leather boots, she could feel the heat rising from the tiled walkways of the fenced garden. What a lovely way to dispel the perpetual chill in her bones from nearly always being indoors!

Beyond the fence, a soft breeze rustled the glistening leaves of the eucalyptus trees, silencing the song of the birds and drawing her gaze toward them.

She saw him—peering at her through the lance-like bars of the fence. She pressed her lips together to quell the cry of surprise that would have otherwise escaped. She noticed he had respectfully taken off his laborer's hat and held it against his chest, as if to conceal his beating heart, she fancied.

He extended his arm through the bars, offering her the small bouquet of purple flowers nestled in velvety green leaves and tied with twine.

Looking fixedly at the flowers, she wondered if she dared accept.

In mute distress, her eyes met his—they were so like her own!

He nodded, coaxing her to take his flowers.

Suddenly aware that she had forgotten to breathe, she relaxed her lips and they began to tingle to the beat of her fluttering heart. She rose from the edge of the pond; instinct whispered to her to make sure her brothers were not looking out of the window, but she did not. The time of day dictated they be in the manor's library, tending to important business matters.

His rough fingers grazed the top of her hand as she took the flowers, sending a forceful shudder through her, almost obliterating his words.

"I will wait for you by the iron gate," he said.

The short sentence flitted in her ears and ran riot inside of her—his gravelly voice caressed her, the tight country folk dialect at once thrilled and

15

mortified her. At nineteen, his was the first male voice she'd heard speak, directly to her, that was not her kin. It never occurred to her it would be the last and only one.

She ducked back in the house, clutching the flowers to her chest, chased by his last pronouncement:

"Midnight."

Terrified that his words might be echoing throughout the entire house for her brothers to hear, she took refuge in her room; only there was she able to settle down. Dreamily, she threaded the alfalfa flowers in the braid of black hair coiled at the base of her neck. A furtive smile played on her lips, knowing that his voice was a frightening, delicious secret for her, and her alone, to keep.

Then it was night.

* * * *

My paternal grandfather passed away circa 1944, leaving his wife and five children at the mercy of his three brothers and two sisters; they were a closed group of people whose strict traditions echoed colonial times of long ago.

Being the youngest of the five orphans, the only home my dad had known was the farm they'd been raised on. The reluctance with which they had to leave it weighed heavily on his heart from then on, but they had no choice; they must live in the city where the family could look after them properly.

Dreading the stuffy life his domineering relatives had mapped out for him, my father broke ranks with the family as soon as he was old enough. Around 1956, he left Ecuador in search of adventure and a place where he might be able to breathe on his own.

Over the next decade, contact with the aunts and uncles was minimal compared to the slightly more frequent correspondence with his mother and siblings. He communicated events as they transpired, letting the family in on his becoming a citizen of the United States, and on meeting and marrying my mother; their move from New York to California, and of course, that they had my two sisters and me.

By return post from his mother and siblings, among the scarce news they considered worthy of committing to a page, he had learned that one of the old aunts, the one that never married, suffered a stroke, just two years after he left. She was only sixty years old, the poor dear, and having lost all mobility and speech capability, she was bedridden. Her brothers duly kept her alive though, as they couldn't bear the thought of losing the pure-hearted, virginal sister whose entire existence had been devoted to looking after her siblings, and her nieces and nephews. The letters implied how much she would love to meet his young family, even if she couldn't embrace them or speak to them.

We had been settled in Los Angeles County for a couple of years when two of my dad's uncles came to see us, in 1967. One of them was very ill, and the other, on behalf of the family, was there to seek the opinion and skill of a foreign doctor.

Back home in Ecuador, fretfully awaiting their return, were the third uncle and two aunts.

Sadly, the many hopes pinned on a successful medical intervention in California came to naught, and the surviving brother would have to return to Ecuador, alone.

It was the day before his departure and still, no phone call had been made, no letter had been sent to convey the sad news to those waiting for him.

It became clear to my father that his uncle was not equal to the task; he simply could not fathom being the bearer of such tragic tidings. Instead, counting on his own authority over my dad and the rest of the family, and easing his conscience that by withholding the truth he would spare unimaginable pain to his remaining brother and sisters, he concocted a story in which a prolonged treatment to improve the serious condition of their brother had been necessary. My father would, of course, be at hand in California to monitor the life-saving therapy.

Thus, my father's uncle returned to Ecuador, and his tall tale held up for several years, mostly because the family would not dream of questioning their brother. Their suspicions and doubts about the tragic reality must have festered with every unanswered letter and while waiting for the long-distance calls that never came. Still, not one of them dared ask the question that must have certainly been burning in all their hearts: "When did he die? ...that we might at least commemorate the date."

* * * *

1969

For reasons known only to himself, my dad decided to go back to Ecuador. He knew full well our return could not be broadcast to his extended family because it would force answers to long-suppressed questions.

He transplanted us anyway, from our Los Angeles home to an abandoned groundskeeper dwelling adjacent to his uncle's large manor. I was three years old when we arrived at this new, far-flung home—about an hour by car from Quito, the capital city of Ecuador.

It was explained to us, the children, that we were to remain hidden whenever my dad's uncles came to check on the closed-up manor, which would be every few weeks.

To my mother, it must have seemed as if we had traveled back in time, from suburban LA to a remote post with no running water and no electricity. But she accepted it and her stoic approach set the tone for us kids.

Our new home had been built on a slope, over 130 years before, by a family long extinct when we got there. The stone walls of the first story were a partially subterranean enclosure to a series of four stalls, which my mother assumed had been used to keep animals, and to store alfalfa hay and tools.

We lived upstairs, where there were two bedrooms, a bathroom, kitchen and sitting room. My sisters and I slept in a long room where our three twin beds were lined up, one after the other. Our housemaid's bed was wedged at the very end of the room, by the window overlooking the dirt road on which donkeys and indigenous people passed on foot, to and from their homes in the nearby hills.

Shortly after we had settled in, the night-time visits began.

I don't remember the exact conversations, but as I lay there waiting for my nightly voyage into dreamland to start, a sweet lady would sit on my bed. She would ask me questions I was happy to answer. She shared tales using mostly images and few words, but she encouraged me to tell her stories, apparently amused by my high-pitched voice and how fast I spoke.

Inevitably, those conversations would wake the "passenger" on the bed next to mine. When this happened, the disrupted sister would call "Mami!" and I would have to explain that I was speaking with an adult visitor, because that absolved me from fault, and I described the lady in as much detail as I could: her sparkly brown eyes and chocolate skin, her long dark hair, which she sometimes braided and deftly coiled at the back of her neck while she talked with me.

Since my mother's questions about it didn't discourage the connection or signal distress (in my mom's family, coexisting with the supernatural is a natural condition), I took it for granted that the lady visited each of us in turn. It never occurred to me that I might be the only one seeing and hearing her, about once every week.

* * * *

Whether she got bored with me, or she could no longer come see me, the frequency of the lady's visits lessened as I got older, and by the time I was twelve, I'd all but forgotten her.

Perhaps the increased activity and distractions may have had something to do with it too, for in the nine years since our arrival, my mother had changed the groundskeeper dwelling and turned it into a beautiful, two-story country home for us. We still slept upstairs, but now we each had our own room, and the stalls downstairs had been cleaned up and remastered into our living room, formal dining room and spacious kitchen.

The grounds around the house were spectacular, surrounded by rolling hills and gullies prompting us to explore. All manner of trees grew around our place: eucalyptus, fig, walnut, sour orange, pepper, lemon, pine, palm trees with mini coconuts, avocado, you name it! There were also alfalfa fields, my mother's roses, and a vegetable garden near the house. Marking the western boundary of the property was a commercial chicken coop, so efficiently managed by my mother that its profits had financed the improvements done to our home.

To my sisters and me, and our dogs, this was our playground and it afforded us dozens of favorite spots, like the pine grove by the abandoned manor, where on lazy afternoons we became princesses, living in an enchanted forest.

Afraid we'd be led astray by our curiosity, Dad had warned us not to go near the old house.

But how could we help ourselves? Especially me!

As if the sight of the house wasn't enough of a challenge to resist, the warning against it served to entice me beyond caution. I'd often climb over the lance-like bars into the garden, while my sisters kept watch—I may have broken a glass pane or two, hoping to get to the wood shutters, because what if they were unlatched? What if they just opened at my touch? I knew I'd see the sumptuous rooms beyond, cluttered with spindly-legged tables, heavy couches with pillowy cushions, bookshelves crammed with dusty tomes, and canopy beds hung with velvet!

The shutters never budged though, and no such vision ever materialized. Instead, my dad's uncle, who seemed to visit his property less and less every year, had noted the broken glass and notched wood, and he had rightly assumed someone wanted to break in.

Lamenting the fact that the indigenous population seemed to be on the rise, he asked my dad to look into hiring a watchman.

So, my rookie efforts at breaking and entering had become evident at last! My sisters knew, and my dad must've known, I was the culprit, so I ceased and desisted, cold-turkey. But every now and then I'd slip. When the moon was full, I'd climb out of my bedroom window, cross our lawn and then hedge the crop rows on the way to the forbidden house. Our two collies would follow me in silence, humoring me or, perhaps, simply enjoying the moonlight escapades as much as I did.

Despite the shadows playing tricks on me, I'd walk around the manor, silent and focused, checking for that door or window that might have miraculously opened. *Nope. Shuttered tight.* Wondering if, when I died, I'd retrace my steps, and grinning about the certainty that indeed I would, I'd reach the northwest corner of the building. I would grab the iron bars and stare into the moonlit garden, like a prisoner longing to return to her cell.

* * * *

1978

Beckoning moonlight spilled onto my pillow. I unlatched the window, as I'd done so many summer nights before, and climbed out. Holding on to the ledge, I slid carefully until my feet touched the iron window-guard below. I balanced for a moment, pressed against the wall, and then dropped the final few feet to the cement patio behind our house.

Feeling buoyant under the silver moon, I ran up the hill, beyond the chicken coop to The Throne. Long before our family had arrived, someone felled a large eucalyptus tree, though not cleanly, for the trunk appeared to have torn itself from the wide stump, leaving a tall, jagged edge on one side, like a regal backrest. My sisters and I were convinced that this spot marked a magical dimension; we were sure the faerie court gathered there, in the confines of a ring of toadstools, with the enthroned queen as a centerpiece amid the reveling spirits of the wood.

High up in the sky, the moon shone bright, eclipsing the stars around it. As mistress of my domain, I surveyed the landscape below. My gaze settled on the dark mass made up of the old manor and the tunnel of trees leading from the east gate to the main circular driveway. From my vantage point, the manor looked like a bizarre square balloon tethered to its iron gate by the thickest of ropes.

Seemingly of their own accord, my legs bounded downhill; I flew toward the wrought-iron gate as if pulled by a magnet.

I paused at the top of the circular driveway, by the empty cherub fountain. The tree-lined drive stretched before me, shrouded in darkness. I squinted at the iron gate at the end, noting the eerie effect caused by the silvery glow beyond it. My first tentative steps in dappled moonlight soon led me into unbroken darkness, and the tunnel of trees swallowed me.

Although increasingly distressed by the silence, I resisted the impulse to sprint back home. Refusing to be a scaredy-cat, I challenged myself to *first* touch the gate, and only then could I go back home.

Heavy scuffling sounds to my right startled me. I thought perhaps a cow had been left behind on a tether and was trying to break free. Intent on assisting if possible, I inched closer.

Disconcerted and unable to comprehend what was happening, I watched two men viciously attacking a third. When I finally understood, I scrambled to the opposite side of the path and hid behind a tree.

From the relative safety provided by the wide trunk, I stared, gripped again by the violence of the act unfolding before me. A few seconds later, the two men backed away, breathing hard. The third lay on the ground, very still.

One of the attackers tossed a straw hat, which landed neatly on the chest of the body. Then, the two passed a few feet in front of me, headed out of the property in haste. They sidled out of sight through a wide gap between the bars of the gate—I'd never noticed that big of a gap before.

When I could no longer see or hear them, I came out of my hiding place and crossed the path to see about the man they'd left behind.

From beneath the hat, a dark mass spread slowly outward, staining his white shirt.

The shocking realization of what that stain was, as much as the sudden awareness that my dogs were not with me, sparked the long overdue reaction. I spun on my heel and dashed through the trees, berating myself for taking such risks and wondering why in the hell I'd gone there in the first place.

Just get home! I thought frantically, but that only served to make the trees obstruct my progress; they took on the thick, tangled quality of seaweed, swaying in a deep ocean, immobilizing me. I screamed but the sound died at the top of my throat. Mossy arms wrapped tight around my ankles. I thrashed against them but that only worsened my situation.

A last valiant effort allowed me to wrench my arm free and I sat up, meaning to release my legs from the tight bonds. I fumbled in the dark—dizzy, breathless, increasingly panicked until it dawned on me; I was in my room, tangled in my own sheets!

Perplexed, I held still, hoping to situate myself in the shadows. Slowly, I found my way back to the head of the bed, and began straightening out the blankets the best I could. I lay back on my cool pillow and gazed at the stars twinkling at me through the gap in the curtains.

On my right, I felt the covers tighten slightly with the weight of someone sitting beside me. A forgotten, though familiar, voice whispered, "A long-gone nightmare, sweet girl."

Relief washed over me like a soothing potion, and my heart settled down. Body and mind relaxed, and the night's exertions diluted to nothing in deep slumber.

* * * *

1984

In less than three weeks I'd be a high school graduate, and I would be returning to California at long last!

What a bittersweet feeling, to leave my parents, my sisters, and the place where I'd been shaped into this preliminary version of myself—but at the same time, how thrilling to be on the brink of the next phase of my life.

In a flurry of excitement, I wondered what might be waiting for me out there. Who would I become? I hadn't the slightest clue, not even through my finest daydreaming effort, but I was ready to take on the new adventure.

Lights had been out for a couple of hours next door, in my sister's room. She was asleep by now for sure.

Through the gap in the curtains, a moonbeam cut a path from my forehead to my belly. I grinned in the dark, accepting the invitation, possibly for the last time in a long while.

I quickly changed out of my pajamas and, with well-practiced skill, climbed out of my bedroom window. At once my dogs were there and we set out to The Throne, because of all my favorite haunts, it afforded the best valley views.

The alfalfa fields were long gone; they'd been replaced with corn a while back, which meant I wouldn't be indulging in a downhill run. I wasn't fussed about that because a walk along the waterway was just as fun, so long as gravity didn't suck me into the muddy bottom of the two-foot-wide channel.

Sitting on the faerie queen's throne, with my dogs on either side of me so I could scratch behind their ears, I got my fill of fresh air while faithfully recording in my mind the image of the moonlit hills, the groves and shrubberies sprawled in dark masses between my home and the old manor, and the various pathways connecting everything.

We started back, single file along the waterway, which was empty because laborers only ran it during the day. Soon we passed the out-of-use chicken coop, and then our house. I turned right, shortly after passing the enormous pepper tree on our lawn and walked over to the northwest corner of the manor.

The caged garden slumbered there, forlorn as ever, like a spinster, and I was suddenly overcome with years of frustration—why did my dad's uncle allow this place to languish like this when he could have had a family love it, care for it, nurture it? We would've prevented brittle vines from scratching the walls with their petrified claws, we would've kept tiles from crumbling and accentuating the garden's derelict appearance. The roof wouldn't be sagging with the weight of decades of neglect.

If given the opportunity, we could have lifted the shroud of melancholy enveloping the whole house. Even now, I knew all it wanted was a family to love it.

Annoyed, I turned away and walked around to the cherub fountain; it was full of debris, of course—I'd never seen it clean, much less with water in it. With a mounting bad temper, I observed the missing pavers on the circular driveway, and as I took the path to the iron gate I noticed that it too was riddled with potholes and cracked slabs.

When I got to the gate, I grabbed the bars, knowing they'd leave rust stains on my palms—who knew when any maintenance had last been done on the property. What a waste!

Uncertain as to whether I had sensed it or seen it out of the corner of my eye, I turned to my right to get a good look at a light-colored something that had caught my attention. A soft breeze made the thing slide out of sight and I chased it. Through narrowed eyes, I saw it had come to rest several feet from the tree-lined drive.

I crept closer.

A laborer's hat!

My mind reeled.

At that moment, a distant voice reached me: "Only a long-gone nightmare, sweet girl." And then, a total recall overtook me; lost memories of bedside conversations, the transcendent happiness a simple bouquet of alfalfa flowers could give, the dead man in my nightmare, the grievous consequences of unbending traditions practiced by selfish hearts. A captive soul's haunting escapades from a dying body.

At my side, the dogs let out a low growl, threatening to start barking soon. "What do you see?" I said, scratching behind their ears. But they looked around impassively, pressing their heads against my palms, like a pair of cats demanding attention.

I glanced at the hat one last time, wondering: If I dug up that spot, would I find a decomposed body—a skeleton?

Both dogs let out warning barks.

I walked away, feeling I would carry that doubt for the rest of my life. "A forgotten nightmare, or maybe a forgotten sin?"

* * * *

1988

News of the death of my dad's aunt, the one that never married, reached me in California. She was ninety years old, and I have no recollection of ever meeting her.

Since her massive stroke not only had she been unable to move or speak, but her organs had been shutting down bit by bit. My mother told me over the phone she had finally succumbed, after years of pointless attempts by her one surviving brother to extend her life.

Up until then, my knowledge of her condition had been vague at best, as such things would never be openly discussed with the children. So, on the occasion of her death, rather than expressing how incomprehensible that generation's behavior was to me, I limited myself to echoing my mom's opinion about the sad business—I pitied the poor lady, because although she'd shown signs of mental fitness to caregivers, the truth about her brother's death, years before, had been cowardly kept from her, along with

23

the news of her nephew's return with his family.

It struck me, then and there, that just like the old manor, she might have enjoyed a family—her family—to love her and, if nothing else, be a means of distraction from the prison her body had become, even if for short spells at a time.

"What torture her life must have been—thirty years a prisoner in her own mind, unable to communicate or do anything for herself," my mom remarked, but as I didn't say anything right away, she added, "When you were little, you used to say a lady came and talked with you at night."

My ears perked up and my senses crackled.

"The way you described her, it sounded just like your dad's aunt, but since she wasn't dead at the time, I decided it couldn't possibly be her visiting you."

I concentrated really hard to see her—it had been such a long time ago and the memories were fuzzy, but she swam into view suddenly, so that at length I said, "She is now at rest, Mami," convinced that it was so, even though we'd never met in person.

Hardly had we wrapped up the call than I slipped, or was swept, into a flight of fancy in which the enticing concept of astral projection was a key factor—and the centerpiece? A sweet lady, a blood relative, who had sat on my bed at night, braiding her long dark hair, telling me her stories, and smiling benignly at my childish tales.

SHE CAUGHT A RIDE

Kelsey E. Gerard

Gone but Not Forgotten

If you dare, go ahead and visit Flo's grave in the Ogden City Cemetery. But, do you know the secret signal?

Zoe expertly wedged the blue Grand Caravan across the narrow Martin Hilltop Drive, inside Ogden City Cemetery. She put the van in reverse and backed up, nearly touching the chain-link fence before it finally rocked into park. Beside her, on the passenger seat, my body still tingled with the now absent vibration of the car and my anticipation of what was to come.

A quick flash of headlights to my left—Jessica parking near us and cutting the engine of her parents' Yukon.

Several headstones stood in the path of light made by our two vehicles. The silence of the blindfolded freshmen in the back seats sent a shiver through me, bringing back memories of my own initiation into the volleyball team.

"Are we okay to block the road like this?" Emily said, snapping me out of my thoughts.

"It's fine. It's late, so I don't think any cops will show up," Zoe replied.

"Emily, turn off your phone. You're ruining the mood," I said, reaching for it impatiently.

She jerked it away. "Really, Cate, *mood?* You mean it's not dark enough for you?" she said dryly, but still smiled and locked her phone.

"Shut up, you two! It's time for freshie initiation." Zoe locked eyes with me and a mischievous grin streaked across her features. "Cate?"

"Right." I got out and opened the sliding door of the van, while Jessica climbed out of her Yukon. The sophomores and juniors, all giggling and talking in whispers, got out and loitered around the cars while Emily and I helped the freshmen out of the van. Grabbing them by their hands or elbows, we lined up the five girls to face the tombstones, their backs to the headlights.

"Ladies," I said, glad to be team captain instead of a trembling freshman again. "Remove your blindfolds, please."

Jen came around from the passenger side of the Yukon carrying a metal bowl filled with folded slips of paper. "Here you go," she said, handing it to me.

"Summer is ending, conditioning is over, and it's the last weekend before school starts, so we are going to have some fun." I said the words as solemnly as I could, to give the occasion an ominous taste.

Despite the summer heat, the bowl felt cold in my hands. I clucked my tongue irritably—*am I really going to spook myself?* The snickering varsity girls briefly distracted me from my unsettling observation, but I shot a dark look their way and they got quiet.

"Now, it's time to ask Flo for her blessing," I announced, letting my gaze rest on each girl for a few seconds, aiming to make all five of them anxious. "Have you freshmen ever heard of Flo?"

I knew I'd succeeded when they began shuffling their feet and wringing their hands.

"No, but I'm guessing she's dead," Ali spoke up, arms crossed but not moving from her central spot in the crescent-moon huddle they had subconsciously made. She was the tallest girl on the team, had flawless skin and long blonde hair, but was on my naughty list for pushing all my buttons—always keeping right on me, every day of conditioning! I know she wants my position next year, after I graduate.

I smirked, "Very observant, Ali." Some of the girls laughed at my smart-ass remark, but Ali scowled. I ignored her. "Emily, want to tell the freshmen who Flo is?"

"Yup." Emily stepped into the light and faced her audience. "Flo, or Florence Louise Grange, died in 1918. She was only fifteen years old, so, about the same age as you freshies." Emily paused for effect. "Now, they say that young Florence had a boyfriend, an older guy her father didn't like much, but because she was in love, she would sneak out every night to see him anyway."

"Sounds like your life, Jessica, does that mean you're going to die?" Ali laughed unkindly.

Even though I couldn't see her face, I knew Jessica was rolling her eyes as she replied, "Ha ha, you're funny."

"Ladies," I scolded, staring grimly at Ali for a few seconds and thinking, *God, I hope* you *get picked.* "You want to continue the story, Jess?"

She nodded and cleared her throat; the headlights illuminating one side of her face made the rest of her blend and disappear into the darkness. "The story goes that her boyfriend would drive up to her house and flash the lights of his car three times. Florence knew to come out at his signal." Right on cue, a junior who had sneaked back to the Yukon flashed its headlights once.

I saw Ren, one of the quieter freshmen, jump and for the first time that night I felt a twinge of guilt for what we were doing. She was the shortest girl on the team, but her vertical of 21 inches had gotten her a spot. She didn't talk much, though her speed and hitting skills said more than enough. In addition to the guilt, I got an odd feeling that if anyone squealed about tonight it might be her, her dad being a cop and all.

Jessica went on, and I looked away from Ren, still feeling bad but not bad enough.

"In 1918, everyone around town was dying of influenza, and poor Flo, she got it too. Still, on the night of December 29th that year, sick as she was, she waited and waited by her window. But that night, no headlights flashed, and little, sick Florence died waiting by the window."

"Now, it's been said," Jen picked up the narrative, "that if you flash your headlights three times on her grave, Flo will appear and try to get in your car." A devious smile played on her lips as she continued, "Like us, Flo was on her school's volleyball team, but since she was the kind of girl who liked to go out every night, we figure Flo knew how to have fun. So, *we* take it a step further and every year, we draw a name." Jen jutted her chin toward me, and I took the hint.

"Whoever gets picked has to walk to the headstone, and wait there, while we flash the headlights three times, so Flo can give the team her blessing." I paused, noticing how effective our story-telling was—the freshmen stood shoulder to shoulder now, and even Ali's stance seemed less cocky than usual.

"With Flo's blessing no parents will ever know how many parties we go to," Zoe giggled.

"And, like last season, we won't lose any games either," I clarified. "Last year's pick gets to pull names out of the bowl. If your name gets pulled, you are in the cars waiting. And the *last* name called talks to Flo."

"And you really believe all that—" Ali challenged.

"Obviously," I said, gesturing inclusively to our group and surroundings. "This team does all our activities *together*, especially initiation. If you don't want to join, or if any part of this doesn't work for you, maybe you should try track." We stared at each other for a tense moment. I waited her out, until with some muttering, she gave in and looked away.

Glossing over the short confrontation, Jen clapped her hands briskly and announced, "All right, juniors and sophomores come up here with me. Everyone else, go stand together to get picked."

For a moment all I heard was the sound of shoes on gravel, until our positions shifted and the crescent-moon huddle faced the glaring headlights.

"Okay, now, who's ready to meet Flo for us?" Jen said. "Littles, you were it last year, so you draw."

Littles stepped up and reached into the bowl I was holding. "Heidi," she called out, and Heidi nearly sprinted to the van. Some chuckled at her expense; not Ren though.

Maybe it was the bright headlights, but she looked pale to me, and again I was visited by that overwhelming sense of guilt for the anguish Ren seemed to be hiding.

In less than two minutes, though, it was down to Ali and Ren.

"Best of luck, freshmen," I said, suddenly feeling out of breath.

31

Littles smiled as she dipped her hand into the bowl for the last time. While she made a show of scrambling the two bits of paper, I chanted inwardly, *pick Ren, pick Ren.*

Ali straightened up, competitive to the end, while Ren nervously played with a strand of her sandy blonde hair.

"Would you hurry it up?" Ali grumbled, crossing her arms in irritation.

Ren shuddered visibly, looking more nervous than ever.

Littles drew the slip, unfolded it and called out, "Ali."

It seemed to me Littles and Jen squirmed uncomfortably, which reinforced my sense that it might not be a good idea to put Ren through this, but there was no taking it back now.

Looking disconcerted, or perhaps disappointed, Ali's hands balled into fists at her sides. Saying nothing she walked back to the van and climbed in, closing the door behind her.

Meanwhile, Ren had stopped playing with her hair. Wide-eyed, she looked from Littles, to Jen, to me.

"We picked the wrong one!" Littles hissed at Jen.

"You think?" I chimed in under my breath. "Let's hope she doesn't end up calling her parents." I sighed and walked back to the terrified freshman—she looked on the verge of crying.

"All right, Ren, you have to carry the team here," I said, trying the best I could to make light of the outcome. Jessica pulled out the team jersey we had brought for the occasion and handed it to me. "Here, put this on."

Ren teared up, but she nodded as she pulled the jersey over her T-shirt.

Littles joined us. "Don't be scared," she said, hugging Ren. "It's really fast, you walk up to the headstone, we shine the lights three times, and then you're done. It's easy." She let Ren go, smiled reassuringly, and climbed in the Yukon.

I walked Ren along the first row of headstones, toward the corner of the triangle section we were at. "You'll cross here, and Flo's is on the edge of the lawn over there," I said, pointing to the target a few yards ahead. She was shaking. "Are you going to be okay? Someone else can do it if you're scared."

Ren shook her head and a knot formed in my throat. Did she mean she wasn't going to be okay, or that she didn't want someone else to go in her place? She still said nothing, so I put an arm over her shoulders in an awkward half hug. "Hang tight, you'll be fine," I told her.

A chill draft rose from the grass between the tombstones. As I passed, I told Jessica to kill the Yukon's lights and I got in the van.

My eyes were fixed on Ren. She took a step onto the grass and my gaze raced ahead to Flo's headstone, which, for a terrifying moment, appeared blank!

I rubbed my eyes and the illusion vanished, so that when I looked again, the words were still etched on the stone: *Daughter, Florence Louise Grange, Nov. 24, 1903 – Dec. 29, 1918. Gone but not forgotten.*

"Ready?" Jessica yelled, making Ren, *and me*, jump.

I winced, watching her do an ungainly sidestep to avoid the edges of grave markers in her path. How was she going to deal with what was coming next?

"Emily, text Chad," I said under my breath.

"He left his phone in the Jeep. All the guys did." Emily looked worried.

"What's going on?" Ali leaned over the middle seat of the van, keen to cause problems.

"Nothing," I said. "It will be fine."

"Isn't hazing illegal or something?" Ali asked, and I could hear the laughter in her voice. Did she even care that Ren was borderline breaking down?

"This isn't hazing, Ali, because there is no danger of anyone getting hurt. We do it every year—it's a game," I replied, eager to end the conversation.

Ali slumped back into her seat, arms crossed.

Ren took several more steps, and stopped about a foot from the headstone I had pointed out. She looked back, into the van's lights, and nodded to indicate she'd arrived. It hit me again how she must feel; alone in the dark, blinded by the light, unable to see any of us.

I stuck my head out of the window and called out, "You ready, Ren?"

She nodded tensely. I saw her look down at the headstone right before the lights went out, and she was still in the same position when Zoe turned them back on a few seconds later.

Off, and then on again.

Ren's eyes swiveled in my direction as the lights went out for the third time. There was no moon in the sky, only the faint starlight to comfort her.

Seconds seemed to last an eternity. The lights that had just gone out still had me seeing spots—I couldn't see five feet in front of me, let alone where Ren stood. The girls in the back craned their necks or leaned between the front seats trying to see.

I saw something—a green glow, where Ren had been. I opened the van's door and got out, my heartbeat starting to pick up.

Up ahead, a twig snapped. I heard Ren gasp and then her faltering footsteps on the grass. As I rubbed my eyes again, shadows seemed to thin out in the dark and starlight became sufficient as my eyes adjusted.

The smoky green glow was still there; it drifted into Ren's face just before a black mass jumped out of nowhere and pinned her to the ground.

Ren's scream echoed in the darkness, causing time to resume its normal pace.

I lunged toward her.

Behind me, the headlights flicked on and I heard car doors opening as the others scrambled out to see what had happened. A quick glance over my shoulder confirmed they were too chicken to set foot on the grass and risk stepping on a grave.

"Happy initiation, freshman!" shouted a male's voice, pulling off his black hood to reveal an attractive boy, much older than Ren. "Hey, are you okay?" He crawled off her and knelt beside her as she sobbed. "I'm sorry, please don't cry. It was just a prank," he said, patting her shoulder awkwardly.

I fell to my knees on Ren's other side. "Just get outta here, Chad!"

"I didn't mean to make her cry!" Chad said angrily as he got to his feet and backed away.

She was now in a fetal position. I bent over her. "Are you okay?" I asked in a low voice, trying to sound soothing.

Ren sat up, sniffling and wiping away her tears with the back of her hand. I scanned her face, convinced that the whole thing may have been too much for her.

"Ren?" I pressed, starting to feel worse and worse with every tear that slipped down her face. "It was just a little pre-season fun. I'm so sorry, I couldn't text the guys in time to tell them not to jump out at you."

"Sorry for crying," Ren said, sniffling and hugging herself tightly as if chilled to the bone. She looked up at me and a flicker of green shone in her pupils, like an animal's eyes.

I fell on my butt with a gasp. What the hell was that?

Shaken, I checked her again—normal black pupils set in warm brown irises, not reflecting anything. Chad started laughing. I turned toward him so quickly my neck cricked, but I glowered at him, "Just shut up, and help us up, will you?"

He pulled a face but said, "Sure."

Chad offered his hand to Ren first, as she was the more distressed damsel between the two of us.

She looked away demurely, probably blushing, but still took his hand.

I stood up before he offered to help me. I wiped away the bits of grass that had gotten on my shorts, and putting my arm around Ren's shoulders, I led her back to the van.

"Everything okay?" Jessica shouted from the Yukon.

"Yeah. Yeah, everything is fine, Chad's just a jerk," I replied.

The other girls giggled as they got back into their respective cars and I turned in time to see Chad had thrown his arms up in defeat.

"I just did what you guys told me to," he said, shoving his hands into his pockets. Soon, a couple of other boys in black hoodies came out of the shadows laughing.

"Party at Peterson's house!" the bulkier one shouted. The others seemed to be on board with the idea and Chad hopped into the topless yellow Jeep that had just pulled up next to the Yukon.

"Cate! Ren! Let's go!" Zoe called from the van.

I took Ren's hand; it was so cold that my initial impulse was to let go. But I didn't, and I dragged her with me to the car, trying not to think about her icy fingers.

Zoe turned up the music and the girls in the back sang unapologetically loud to *Demi Lovato*.

The road to the valley snaked before us; the Jeep led the way, followed by the Yukon, and we brought up the rear in the van. At certain turns in the canyon, I could hear the bass pumping out of our windows, back to us and out into the summer night.

Slowly regaining my composure, I rolled down the window and pulled down the sun visor to use the mirror. I tilted my chin up to put on some lipstick.

A flash of green drew my full attention to the bottom left corner of the mirror. Ren's animal-like reflective eyes were fixed on me. She smiled, and for a moment, her face looked like someone else's—an entirely different person, her features clouded by a green haze.

I choked down the yelp that came to the top of my throat and quickly flipped the visor back up. Turning slowly, I stared at Ren's face, now serious and completely her own. *I'm losing my mind!*

"Happy initiation," she said. "Thanks for the ride."

I broke out in goosebumps and my blood turned to ice in my veins.

The green glimmer pulsed again as Ren turned away from me. She leaned her head against the window and smiled up at the stars.

Factual tidbit about *She Caught a Ride*:

Florence Louise Grange was born on November 24th, 1903, in Ogden. She was the second child born to Dottie Susan Mumford and Ralph Manton Grange. Most called her by her middle name, Louise, and not Florence or Flo.

From what little information is available, it seems like she was a well-liked girl. There were a couple of mentions of her being a guest at various parties and she was on a school volleyball team in 1916.

According to Grange family history, the entire family contracted the flu after one of their tenants became ill and brought it into the household. Most of them caught a mild case and didn't spend any time in bed sick. Louise, however, was not so lucky.

Louise caught the flu and died at her home at 5 am on December 29th, 1918 at the age of 15. Her official cause of death was listed as "died suddenly, probably of endocarditis." The contributing factor was influenza. Her death certificate also states she had been sick for ten days.[1]

Daughter
Florence Louise
Grange
Nov. 24, 1903
Dec. 29, 1918.
Gone but not forgotten.

[1] https://www.thedeadhistory.com/flos-grave/

ABIKU

Patricia Bossano

Abiku
Wanderer child. It is the same child who dies and returns
again and again to plague the mother. —Yoruba belief

CHAPTER ONE

April 1999

Matthew, a boy of sixteen, browned by the sun and with eyes the color of a tropical jungle, stood at his desk addressing his classmates in their eleventh-grade anthropology course.

"'Ancient Cultural Myths,'" he said, pulling his sleeves up to his elbows and looking outwardly calm. Despite some lingering nervousness, he managed to steal a few glances toward Joan Anderson, whom he'd never summoned the courage to speak to, though that didn't stop him from fantasizing about her. Matthew's brainy good looks gave him an unapproachable air he wasn't aware of but which caused him to live in relative isolation, perpetuating his ever-present insecurities.

His eyes followed Joan's fingers as she tucked a blonde lock of hair behind her ear, but he looked away before she could notice his glance. Matthew hid his shyness beneath the rehearsed delivery of his report, a tactic that had served him well in the past. He loved language, took pride in using big words and avoided slang wherever possible.

"The Yoruba tribe inhabits western Africa, and their settlements are found mostly in Nigeria." Matthew breezed through the introduction, excited to move on to the meat of his research, which had come from his grandmother's journals.

Shortly after his grandparents married, they had set off on the adventure of a lifetime. Their dream had been to become true inhabitants of the world. They were to spend two years at a time in a different section of the globe so that at a ripe old age they could claim to have seen the entire planet. But it was not meant to be, and they returned to the United States five years after they'd started, having been only to a small portion of Africa.

Soon after they returned, Matthew's grandmother died of cancer, leaving her husband alone to care for their four-year-old daughter, who'd been born among the Yoruba people in Nigeria.

What Matthew knew of his grandmother, which was a great deal, came from the vivid stories told him by his grandfather, stories of remote places in faraway Africa, and of primeval jungles where the eyes of the natural, and the unnatural, watched you every moment of the day. But it was through her handwritten journals that Matthew got a glimpse of the woman his grandmother had been. The journals were given to him, wrapped in brown packing paper and tied with twine, after his grandfather died. They were a token of the love the old man and the young boy had shared for her. Matthew had been ten years old when he received the books.

Late at night in his room, he'd read those old pages and thought he could hear the excitement of his grandmother's thoughts in the sometimes-illegible prose. He felt strangely connected to her. Not only because her blood ran in his veins, but because her words had had the ability to brand fiery visions of savage rituals and sacrifices in his mind, sacrifices that were rational in the minds of the lost tribes she'd lived with, or so she explained in her writings, and Matthew had no trouble following her logic.

After giving his classmates the required geographical bearings of the Yoruba tribe, including local industry and weather references, Matthew launched into a zealous adaptation of a particular experience his grandmother had while living among the Yoruba people.

"The mortality rate of prepubescent children is very high in this tribe," Matthew announced, recalling the various snapshots he'd flipped through the night before of the short months his grandparents had spent with the tribe. He found it satisfying to see with his own eyes the evidence of the statement he'd just made. In the old photographs crowded with natives there seemed to be no more than three or four kids for every twenty adults.

"A high priest explains that the *Abiku* is responsible for the lack of children in their tribe." His classmates gave him a quizzical look and Matthew plowed on with a slight smirk on his face, satisfied with their initial reaction. "An Abiku is a child who dies only to be born again several times to the same mother." The kids in the class shifted in their chairs.

A couple of girls, who'd been whispering and giggling in the back, stopped mid-action to glance in his direction. Those nearest him leaned forward with elbows on their desks supporting their chins on their hands. Matthew pretended he didn't notice any of this, but his eyes now rested inclusively on their faces, his shyness completely gone.

"The term Abiku means several things." He counted them off on his fingers, starting with his thumb, "A reincarnated being. A child who chooses to die, usually before he turns twelve. The spirit realm where an Abiku child comes from. And of course, the spirit itself, with whom it all started."

As he spoke, Matthew could see the pages of his grandmother's journal like a slide-show in his mind. She'd translated the words of the tribe's high priest and entered them as dialogue in her book. Matthew loved the clipped, childlike sentences she'd transcribed. He imagined he could hear the man speaking to her—speaking to him, for that matter.

"The world churns with evil spirits and demons who suffer in their condition outside the physical world," Matthew paraphrased. "They linger like low-hanging clouds over humans, unable to pass into the eternal light. Every minute of the day these spirits wish for the comforts of the living, and some have enough determination to establish contact, usually through a medium or a high priest.

"And so, threatening to wreck their world with his tricks, the evil spirit convinces the medium to satisfy his wants. The priest, anxious to avoid damaged property, spoiled crops, or his people sinking into madness, sets up a series of rituals to appease the demon."

Judging by the pairs of eyes riveted on him, Matthew knew he'd reeled them in good. He allowed himself a satisfied, fleeting grin. His green eyes flashed with anticipation of his classmates' reaction to what came next.

"One such demon is Abiku," he said, becoming suddenly aware of how many times in the past five minutes he'd said the name, "Abiku," a name he'd only read to himself before, but never actually pronounced out loud. He shrugged imperceptibly at this and went on. "Abiku has an insatiable taste for the pleasures of the flesh, so it's no surprise the meager sacrifices of fruit and game offered by the tribe couldn't satisfy him."

A picture of his grandmother beside the old Yoruba high priest flickered into his mind as he spoke. She—tall, blonde, and with a radiant smile on her face. He—about a foot shorter, dark as night but with white hair that looked like a helmet on his head, and a broad toothless grin that made Matthew like him at once.

"Of the demons writhing in the spirit realm at any given time, Abiku was the most driven and determined of all. The high priest said that since the days of the first Yoruba man and woman, Abiku circled the newborn tribe like a hungry hyena, growing more and more dissatisfied with the measly sacrifices they gave him. He wanted *more*." Here Matthew paused for effect, then, in a deeper tone he added, "*Always* more."

He saw Joan squirm in her seat, a slight frown wrinkling her forehead, and Matthew's brow went up knowingly. He'd reacted the same way the first time he'd read this story in his grandmother's book.

"The first Yoruba high priest who heard his moaning pleas was long gone, but Abiku made sure the chain of fear continued from one priest to the next. He needed to secure his sustenance.

"Until the day came, when in greedy desperation, Abiku conceived the notion of stealing a body for himself. If he could commune with a medium, why could he not remain inside it?" The rustling sound of students shifting in their seats filled the room momentarily. Pleased with himself, knowing that what came next was even more shocking, Matthew went on.

"Abiku began his work in earnest. What he wanted was to jolt a spirit out of its rightful body, so he could inhabit it himself. But the high priests were too cunning for Abiku and would not allow such a thing, so his sights turned on the innocent tribe, on its simple members."

Even the teacher, who'd been grading papers while Matthew spoke, appeared to be listening now.

"Abiku followed a woman on her way to the creek early one morning. As she bent to fill her pail, Abiku willed himself through her skin." Joan let out a little gasp at this and Matthew's eyes bored appreciatively into hers. A girl right in front of him shuddered and hugged herself.

"He aimed to possess the woman, but her spirit rejected him like a lioness protecting her cubs. Just as Abiku was about to fracture and disperse in disappointment, the vibrant sound of another beating heart drew him. It turned out the woman was pregnant, you see, and much to the demon's surprise, nothing was so easy as jolting the little spirit out of its incomplete body…"

Matthew stopped. A pressure like a lead apron abruptly settled over him. His heart thumped dully in his chest as he finished his sentence, feeling a little winded, "…Abiku had found his gateway into the physical world."

He swallowed hard and shook his head, hoping to clear his ears and dispel the image that popped into his mind. But it had been so clear! Like he'd seen it right outside his classroom window:

…Mounds of dark pewter clouds gathered to form a gaping mouth. A mouth that devoured a helpless, frightened woman. A woman who looked too much like his grandmother.

He cleared his throat, feeling spooked. He told himself he shouldn't be buying into his own supernatural stories.

"Abiku took over the fetus and thrived on the nourishment of the mother's placenta," Matthew continued; his head twitched once more as he rejected the thought of that gaping mouth. "He was born, and he nursed at the breast of the woman. He grew into an energetic boy who consumed everything in sight. But as the boy's body approached puberty, it seemed to slow down, to settle into an even-keel existence. Abiku didn't like this. It was time to dispose of it and move on to the next vessel."

Feeling slightly sick, Matthew put his fists on the desk and bowed his head. A couple of knuckles cracked. He half shook his head, then straightened up and stubbornly cast about for anyone's face to focus on. His eyes passed over Trent Morgan, who seemed intent on folding a piece of paper for table football. Matthew took a deep breath and his eyes found Joan again. He blinked and said, "The little spirit whose body Abiku had stolen lingered nearby, growing jealous and bitter over the theft. And when Abiku returned to the spirit world leaving the youthful carcass behind, the little spirit grudgingly became Abiku's first companion."

The picture of the toothless Yoruba high priest appeared crisp and unexpected in Matthew's mind, further unsettling him.

The man threw his cottony head back and laughed uproariously at the swirling black clouds above.

Matthew cocked his head to one side and rubbed his eyes absently. "Over the centuries, and after countless such possessions, Abiku proved to himself over and over that exiled spirits were like an extension of himself; they were tethered to him for good.

"It didn't take long either for him to learn he could send these youthful spirits into fetuses or young children and still experience the carnal pleasures his minions enjoyed, as if they were sinister limbs of his. Abiku thought this was more fulfilling than executing the possessions himself, because he was benefiting from the compounded experience of many."

Trent Morgan glanced up at him, the paper football shuffling between his wiggling fingers, and again Matthew paused; his grandmother's writing, her actual thoughts on Abiku's discovery, came to his mind unbidden.

It is a new age for Abiku, she'd written. Gone are his archaic notions that a child should be sacrificed to him, that the high priest should drink its blood so Abiku might experience the heat of the blood. Although that was how Abiku initially secured a high priest to himself: through the sacrifice of a child. How else could the blood pass into the demon, if not through his devoted priest?

Matthew did not mention this to his classmates. What he'd told them so far seemed more than enough for the moment.

"To those who have seen him, Abiku is a creature made up of nothing but smoke. It is said the intangible monster has no stomach, and that is why he hungers forever.

"Forever he tries to satisfy his cravings, only he never will, because no matter what he consumes, it can never become a true part of him."

Although his shyness had left him, his muscles continued to stiffen and distend with each mini-vision popping up in his head. He felt exhausted. It didn't help either that every time his eyes swept over the room, Matthew saw Joan's rapt expression fixed on him. He buried his excitement and confusion over this in the penetrating glances he directed at the other spellbound faces around him.

But through the open blinds of the classroom windows—

The pewter clouds swirled angrily, the gaping mouth dissolved in flashes of lightning. A wicked wind rose out of nowhere, ripping apart the thatched roofs of a dozen huts. Men and women ran for cover, their backs bent, their arms shielding their heads against the storm.

Matthew squinted at the windows. The southern California sun shone out there like any other day. No trace of a storm. *What the hell?*

"Life in the Yoruba tribe, to this day, revolves around keeping an Abiku away, or discovering an Abiku child that might have been born." Matthew stood up straighter and grabbed the back of his neck with his hand, a quick stretch after standing tense for almost fifteen minutes—his hand was cold, and his neck was hot and sweaty. He wiped his hands surreptitiously on his jeans.

"It is said songbirds distract the focus of an Abiku and keep him at bay. That is why every hut in a Yoruba village has cages with the colorful creatures singing at all hours.

"But the cunning Abiku who's managed to be born relishes the battle to remain undetected by his mother. Most of the time, his parents will not discover him until the cruel Abiku child dies within months from birth, or at times, after an entire decade." Matthew made a curt bow.

Everyone applauded, and he shot a goofy, relieved grin at Joan. She clapped more vigorously than anyone and smiled, casting her eyes down in a most promising way.

With a toasty feeling in his belly, Matthew looked away, a grin still playing on his mouth.

For the third time, he noticed Trent Morgan.

Matthew's green eyes locked on Trent's gray ones. And that's when it happened.

A jagged bolt of lightning pierced the swirling mass of murky clouds. All hell broke loose. The wind howled, stripping the huts to nothing but naked frames. The cries of the natives rent the air. And the gaping mouth reshaped itself, except now it had eyes also, two smoldering holes under a smoky brow.

Through Matthew, those smoldering eyes fixed upon Trent.

CHAPTER TWO

This is Trent Morgan, Matthew thought, unnerved as Trent continued to stare at him.

The transfixed expression on Trent's face was that of someone who'd had a revelation.

Holy smokes, thought Matthew, unable to look away and beginning to worry about the silence stretching between them—but could his speech really have had such an impact?

Trent Morgan was the coolest guy in school. He had the face, he had the body and the smarts. Trent had everything, even money.

The toasty feeling Joan's smile had produced in Matthew cooled under Trent's unexpected notice. It didn't cross Matthew's mind that Trent may have been privy to the bizarre visions plaguing him through his oral report.

Matthew had never seen Trent this close before, so he took a really good look at the guy while, with a furrowed brow, he remembered a handful of snippets he'd overheard in the hallways, uttered by giggling, breathless girls: "Oh! I wanna run my fingers through that long hair of his!" and "Mouth like his? He has to be a great kisser!"

His eyes narrowed. With a guy like Trent prowling the hallways, what chance did someone like Matthew have of getting noticed?

"That was good," said Joan as she walked past him on her way out of the classroom, her books held tight against her chest.

Matthew's stomach dropped, and his heart rate soared. He gave her a startled nod and would have thanked her, but the gray eyes were still on him. Out of the corner of his eye, Matthew saw Joan walk out the door and fleetingly wondered if he'd disappointed her by not replying. He half shook his head, annoyed with himself, but his glance flashed back to Trent.

"Definitely more to you than I thought," Trent said, his engrossed expression shifting to a broad welcoming grin. "I like the way you think, man." Trent punched Matthew's arm, and Matthew nearly smiled in confused surprise at finding himself treated with such familiarity.

For two years they'd attended the same school yet moved in completely different circles—with a student body of almost three thousand, that wasn't hard to do. Trent was the football star with a 4.0, and a long line of aspiring girlfriends trailing behind him. Matthew was an inconspicuous 4.0 whose love interest was a Honda 250 and the dusty open desert where he dreamed of a girl like Joan.

I like the way you think. Trent's words echoed in Matthew's mind and the corners of his mouth twitched. But he didn't smile. "I think. Period," he retorted dryly, and Trent laughed his approval.

"That's right! You do!" Trent said, glancing over at Kyle, Nick and Chris, the guys who usually hung out with Trent. Besides the five of them, no one else was left in the history classroom. It was the end of the day.

Trent put his strong brown hand on Matthew's shoulder and they both laughed at the slight directed at the other three.

Matthew guessed Trent had nothing in common with them other than their buff good looks. *He hangs out with them because he likes the girls' reaction at the sight of them,* Matthew thought, and again he sagged a little, considering his own wiry frame so lacking in developed musculature.

It was obvious Trent wanted some challenging company for his brain, and Matthew flattered himself that was the reason for Trent's choosing to acknowledge him. A deep sense of loyalty surged in him at the possibility, and it would persist for months to come.

Their friendship took off and Matthew's life pitched into fast-forward mode. In between Trent's football games and practices, the two of them were joined at the hip. Matthew found himself energized and motivated. Trent introduced him to a world of unprecedented physical exertions he hadn't even thought of taking on.

Matthew loved it. Everything was extreme with Trent: surfing, skateboarding, paint-balling, dating, and Matthew pushed himself to keep up. He relished the challenge and the avenues Trent opened for him, all the while hoping it wasn't obvious to everyone he sometimes struggled with Trent's pace.

His peers suddenly saw Matthew in a new light, that of Trent's superman reputation. Within days after that history session, girls began to view Matthew's awkwardness as an enticing quality, and paired with his natural though somewhat lanky good looks, Matthew became quite the item.

Though he knew a few girls exchanged notes with each other about him, much to his dismay his new buddies seemed to have divided him from Joan. Sure, he was appreciative of the fact that Joan didn't react to Trent like other girls, but did she need to include Matthew in her avoidance tactics?

Despite it all, Matthew remained the same soft-spoken, determined kid he had always been. He still walked with his hands in his jean pockets because he thought his knuckles protruded unbecomingly; he avoided eye contact wherever possible, as he didn't care to speak to people he didn't know. In short, even amid his newfound popularity, he struggled with his old shortcomings.

Trent became a welcome fixture in Matthew's life and he considered himself a lucky young man. But things changed.

The day came when Trent, who'd never been high on anything but adrenaline and endorphins, confessed to Matthew he'd snorted his first line. As weeks went by, and as much as Trent claimed he was just experimenting, Matthew had a sneaky suspicion Trent might be in over his head with cocaine.

Trent never did anything halfway, it was always to the extreme, and Matthew worried about him. Trent had become a brother to him, a role model, and Matthew hated seeing him make wrong choice after wrong choice. So, he militantly envisioned Trent turning himself around, refusing to believe he'd stay on the path he'd chosen. But by the end of the school year, their time together had become a series of interventions on Matthew's part to tone down Trent's explosive behavior. There seemed to be so much of it lately, Matthew was at a loss for ways to curb Trent's inclinations, and they arrived at their inevitable first confrontation.

Matthew's humiliation over Trent catching on to his attraction for Joan developed into anger when Trent began making the advances Matthew never dared. Only mildly did it pacify him that Joan rejected the abrasive attempts.

* * * *

June 1999

Joan and two of her friends arrived at one of the many wild parties Trent organized at Kyle's house. Light poured from every window and music blared out in rumbling waves over the lawn.

A sinking feeling overwhelmed Matthew when he saw her walk into the crowded living room. *It's my fault and nobody else's,* he told himself. *If I weren't such an idiot, Joan would be my date tonight… She would've been my girlfriend for months now, if I had the nerve…* Matthew tried his best not to sulk. *There's no way I can talk to her with him here.*

Matthew kept his eyes on Trent, becoming more and more troubled by his behavior. Gone were the days when girls longed for Trent's attention. Of late, it seemed he frightened them with his demands, which of course irked him and made him even more hostile.

With the shot-glass he'd just emptied still in his hand, Trent stumbled toward Joan. Matthew stiffened and inched closer as well.

"Don't you look hot tonight," he slurred, giving her a thumbs-up.

Matthew bit back a grin when he saw the scathing glance Joan rewarded Trent with. She turned back to her friends with a dignified toss of her hair.

"Hey, I said you look hot…" Trent insisted, a drunken smirk on his face.

Joan didn't pause in her conversation with her friends. Matthew figured she meant to ignore him. *No good.* He braced himself.

Trent grabbed her arm and whipped her around to face him. "I paid you a compliment," he said in a dangerous tone.

"Get your hands off me!" Joan cried, looking outraged.

In two strides Matthew was right behind Trent. He put his hand on his shoulder. "Hey, man…"

"Fuck off!" Trent growled, and sent Matthew staggering backwards with a shove.

It took Matthew a few seconds to regroup from Trent's hot-headed reaction. Seconds during which he heard Joan scream, "You're a jerk, you know that?" He saw tears gleaming in her eyes.

"But you still want a piece of this." Trent flashed a malevolent grin, dropping the shot-glass and forcing Joan's hand to his crotch.

Joan raised her free hand to slap him, but Trent caught her wrist midair.

"We can do rough, if you want," he slurred, squeezing her face, none too gently, between his thumb and the rest of his fingers.

To Matthew it was like a bad dream taking place in slow motion. Around them, nobody seemed to notice what was going on. He couldn't tell if it was the bass or his heart rattling his rib cage.

He grabbed Trent's arm and pulled him around, which gave Joan the opportunity to free herself from his grip. She raced out of the house in a rage, followed by her two friends. Matthew wanted nothing more than to go after her, but the look of loathing she'd given him stopped him. The look said, *why do you hang out with this asshole?* It was the very thing Matthew had been asking himself for several weeks now.

"What's your problem, Matt?" Trent spat, pushing on Matthew's chest with both hands.

"What's MY problem? What's YOUR problem? Don't you realize what a jerk you're being?"

"Get over yourself, man, you pussy-foot around her like she's a princess! And honestly, I thought you'd be more appreciative…"

"What the hell are you talking about?"

"I was going to share—it's not like I wanted her for myself…" Trent sneered, not the slightest tone of contrition in his voice.

"Have you gone off your rocker?" Matthew shook his head and backed away, disgusted. He instantly thought better of it though and stomped back with an angry scowl. "You've crossed the line, Trent, can't you see that?" He bored into the gray eyes, hoping to see admission or remorse for what he'd done, but there was nothing. "Can you even see yourself?"

"Matt, c'mon. Chill, man! I was just trying to speed things up…"

Matthew threw his arms up in the air and rolled his eyes.

"How long was it going to take you to make a move on her? Huh? Get real, will ya? They're there for the taking," Trent said, jerking his chin toward the room at large. Then he ran his hands over his face in a tired fashion and with a nasty smirk he added, "Besides, Abiku wants what he wants…"

For a few thunderstruck seconds, the statement hung in the air like a rancid smell. Matthew tried to say something but couldn't. For a moment, all he could see was the cotton-headed high priest, bent over with laughter.

Trent laughed at Matthew's stunned silence and put his arm around him. "I was just trying to show you how it's done."

"What do you mean, *he wants what he wants*?" Matthew demanded.

"Who?" Trent grinned, punching Matthew on the shoulder. "I got this, bro, I'll get her for you…"

Repelled, Matthew swatted Trent's arm and stood squarely in front of him. "I don't want you getting anything for me!"

Trent's smile faded, then flat-out disappeared, as he made a clarification that struck Matthew as sinister. "*I said*, not to worry. We'll get her for you, my friend."

Slack-jawed, Matthew stared at Trent. He couldn't shake the disgust he felt. Everyone in the room continued to have a good time; to them nothing had happened. If they'd seen it or heard it, they didn't seem to think it contemptuous.

Whatever the case, Matthew realized, a line was crossed that never should have been messed with.

CHAPTER THREE

For the entire week following the party, Matthew's thoughts alternated between hating, pitying, and feeling hopeful for Trent. He wished he could forget the whole incident. After all, Joan seemed to be okay and had thanked him for his attempt to help, but even during that exchange, Matthew could tell his chances with her had dimmed because of her obvious censure. Joan disapproved of Trent and it followed, in Matthew's mind, she didn't approve of him either.

She doesn't know him like I do. He's having it rough for now, said Matthew's enduring sense of loyalty toward Trent. But the dissonant reference to Abiku crept into his mind as if to help Joan's cause; yeah, why the hell would he say a thing like that, *Abiku wants what he wants—*

Matthew couldn't give up on Trent, so he needed to get to the bottom of that. "He can be saved," he muttered.

Even though Trent still showed no remorse, and even though two weeks had passed, Matthew admitted with a degree of hope that he seemed a little like his old self. Trent had laid off the drugs for a few days in a row, at least in front of the boys, and Matthew saw this as a small ray of hope in the crumbling relationship he was trying to salvage.

* * * *

August 1999

Three weeks before the new school year kicked off, Trent began football practices and Matthew saw him take to the grueling daily routine with the same physical drive of old. Yet another silver lining.

But they hadn't been back to school one week when Trent corralled them in a far corner of the parking lot after practice. There, he showed them the funny little papers he'd gotten his hands on.

Kyle, Chris and Nick, the rest of the *squadron* as Trent called them, didn't hesitate to try them.

Matthew thought better of it. He'd smoked the grass, he'd drunk tequila, but harder core? That was not for him. Matthew hung back and watched them. He tried not to spoil their fun and humorously thought of himself as the designated sitter.

They stumbled about, following whatever psychedelic feast their minds cooked up. He helped them up when they tripped and fell on their faces, and he stretched on the grass with them as the effects of the trip wore off. He listened with an amused smile on his face as they tried to explain what they'd seen and felt.

He didn't envy them; just looking at their clammy, pale faces made Matthew glad he hadn't joined in.

From then on, the boys shared the LSD feasts when Trent bought, but Matthew knew that was the extent of their consumption. The squadron members could not afford it, whereas Trent never seemed to have cash flow problems.

All in all, Matthew thought it was a manageable situation; in fact, he felt pretty good to be the one who looked after them. He was sure they'd grow out of it, or at least get tired of it soon.

The problem was that with each refusal to party, no matter how honorable and responsible Matthew's reasons were, he had to meet the expression in Trent's eyes, an expression revealing a deep-rooted resentment Matthew didn't feel he deserved.

CHAPTER FOUR

May 2000

The afternoon sun spilled its sparkling rays over Santee, a young community bordering the city of San Diego.

Not twenty miles from the Pacific, Santee boasted new houses and shopping centers. A soft breeze cooled the mid-May heat and on Summer Crest Lane, children squealed with laughter as they ran through sprinklers on their lawns. A couple of girls in skimpy shorts and bikini tops sprayed themselves and the car they were washing, on a driveway free of oil stains or cracks.

The normal sounds of this tranquil neighborhood soared in the air and through the open windows of a white split-level home with cheery forest-green shutters and front door to match.

Inside, Matthew, now seventeen years old, his long-limbed body sprawled on the couch, stared at the ceiling. He could hear the voices of parents calling their children in for lunch and grinned dolefully at the high-pitched complaining that followed. He thought how, forever ago, that had been him and his younger sister.

Despite it being a warm afternoon, Matthew felt chilled in his family room. He didn't want to call it *fear* just yet. For weeks, he'd been wrestling with suspicions and conjectures, unable to come to a satisfying conclusion, plus the increasing inability to enjoy things that had amused him in the past irritated him no end. More and more his thoughts drifted toward blaming Trent for his discomforts.

The sudden ringing of the phone jolted him from his reverie. The anxiety he'd been trying to get rid of sprang anew inside of him.

"I'll get it!" Samantha said, racing to the phone.

Matthew sat up on the couch and ran his fingers through his short hair. He knew the call was for him.

"Yeah?" she said into the mouthpiece.

Matthew couldn't hear the voice on the other end of the line, but he could see Samantha rolling her eyes and clenching her jaw. Matthew swallowed hard. He should've disconnected the phones in the house.

"Just a sec," she said dryly, and without bothering to cover the mouthpiece, she called out to him as if he were upstairs rather than a couple of feet away, "Matt! It's that bonehead friend of yours!"

A surge of irritation for his sister's reckless remarks made Matthew jump off the couch infuriated.

"Geez, Sam, will you shut up?" he hissed at her. "Get out of here… Now!"

Samantha grinned, further antagonizing him. *She has no idea just how bad Trent's gotten*, he thought grimly.

"Can I help it if you don't know how to choose your friends?" she cooed, though her eyes were cold on his. Samantha had only seen Trent twice, and that had been enough for her to tell her brother to "just ditch the jerk," but Matthew laughed off her irrational dislike of his friend. "Dream on," he had told her months before, and she'd given up the cause, but her taunting attacks on Matthew and on Trent, whenever she had the opportunity, continued with no signs of relaxing.

Samantha tossed the phone at him and headed upstairs.

Matthew groaned. Like it or not, his sister had been clever enough to sense something was wrong with Trent. From the very beginning, Samantha had perceived his propensities and had disliked him at once. He couldn't deny that the Trent who'd befriended him a year ago was long gone.

The littlest thing could set off this new Trent, and who could say what would happen this time? Matthew didn't have a clue. The last thing he needed though was for his thoughtless sister to get herself in the middle of it.

"Trent?" Matthew said into the phone, his tone apologetic, determined to make peace.

"I'll pick you up at four-thirty, so be ready to go."

Trent's preoccupied tone, and that he'd let Samantha's rude comment slide without a threat, further unsettled Matthew. He fumbled for words but all he came up with was: "Uh…"

The line went dead.

Matthew sagged back onto the couch, clicked the OFF button on the phone and dropped it on the carpet. He laid his head on the armrest and tried to convince himself everything would somehow turn out fine.

He's probably playing one of his stupid games. He'll get us all out there for some jacked-up initiation and then he'll laugh his head off once he knows we're all freaked out and ready to lose it. That's so like him—to get us all worked up and then laugh in our face. But more than that? He won't. He can't do anything.

He noted the time: one o'clock in the afternoon. *Only three and half hours to go*, Matthew thought and, in his mind, the bony shoulders of the Yoruba priest with the cottony head shook with laughter.

CHAPTER FIVE

Matthew couldn't stop mulling over the changes he'd seen come over his friend. He could almost understand how someone like Trent would make a conscious decision to start doing drugs, "just for the experience." After all, Trent's approach was to try everything at least once. But then not be able to shake it? *He's been at it for months!* Matthew thought wearily.

Matthew had come to realize he'd expected more from Trent than was reasonable, and he'd credited him with strength of character beyond what Trent actually had.

Still on the couch, Matthew rolled over on his side and stared slantwise at the spinning blades of the ceiling fan, feeling mocked by the memory of that fateful day in history class. He'd been so excited to shock his classmates with the spooky tale of a demon. How harmless it had seemed then, yet it sickened him now to think the damned report that brought them together nearly a year ago was the very thing severing what puny ties were left of their friendship.

"The stupid report," he muttered, moving on to a more spine-chilling recollection. Had it already been five months? Just a little over.

Trent had shown up at his house on New Year's Eve morning, and Matthew could tell something was up right away, because they weren't supposed to head out to the desert until dusk—the set plan was to greet the dreaded Y2K with no technology besides motorcycles.

Trent's manic frame of mind immediately put Matthew on his guard. *This isn't a normal high—unless he's been mixing drugs?* Whatever the case, Trent's words and his behavior had put an alien fear in Matthew's heart.

"Abiku, man," he had said, running his fingers through his hair, over and over, seemingly unaware of it.

Something cold clawed Matthew's insides at the mention of the name, Abiku, and he eyed Trent suspiciously as he paced the garage.

"Your bud, from Nigeria… Do you believe it? He's been to see me, man, and he's got plans!"

This is no LSD trip, Matthew remembered thinking that morning, *No, he's finally gone off the deep end.*

"Dude—I think I might become a high priest. That's my calling, man!" Trent let out a vicious laugh that made Matthew's heart jump to his throat. Trent put both hands, vice-like, to his own head like he wanted to squeeze something out of it, but then ran his fingers through his hair again.

It looked to Matthew like Trent would soon jump out of his skin as he continued to pace and gesticulate in the garage, stopping only to pull a square piece of paper from his expensive leather wallet.

Matthew got a sour taste in his mouth and couldn't smooth out the scowl on his face as his eyes followed Trent's strides. "Hey man, you've had enough for one afternoon," Matthew had said, squinting at the LSD square, but a lot of good it did. Trent hadn't even looked up, he just went on with his feverish rant.

"You introduced him to me, Matt, remember?" he'd said, putting the paper under his tongue, laughing and taunting him. "...But you know what? He wants to meet you... He wants to meet all of us, bro! In person!" He threw his head back and whirled with his arms stretched out, laughing, reminding Matthew of the Yoruba priest he'd been seeing in his head so often in the past year.

"You're scaring the crap out of me..." Matthew tried to grin.

Trent laughed even louder but then stopped short as if coming to his senses, or at least to a sense of something being wrong. "He won't leave me alone!" Trent hissed, and his gray eyes gleamed with fear as they darted from one corner of the garage to the other, as if someone had just stepped out but would be back any second.

Fear was something Matthew had never seen in Trent. It lasted only a few seconds, but it had been enough for the idea to take shape in Matthew's mind that something was happening to Trent, and that it had a firm hold of him. Immediate hope ignited in Matthew's heart that maybe, somewhere in his mind Trent might be aware of it. That dwindling sense of loyalty stirred within Matthew once again and the weight of responsibility steeled him; after all, he was the designated sitter. He must pull Trent through this.

Matthew shook off the memory of that day but directly, the fears his grandmother had described in her journals took on a life of their own. Lately, those were the two things occupying his mind and they weighed on him, making it hard to even breathe. When not thinking about Trent's fears, his grandmother's words stabbed his soul with overpowering intensity.

...My own daughter, dear God, she's only two years old.
How could she possibly know?
What have we done?
I did not believe what the high priest told us and now my baby girl is being accosted by this creature.
What have we done?

But it is true then! It must be! Because how, then, could a two-year-old say such things?

"He told me I'm pretty, Momma."

"He wants to come live inside me."

"He says if I let him, I can fly forever in the air, and I won't get mosquito bites anymore, or feel sick to my tummy... Can I, Momma? Can I let him?"

My dearest Joseph agrees with me, we must leave. We must take her away from here and never speak the horrid name again.

Abiku.

Matthew had found the separate sheet of paper hidden in the false cover of one of his grandmother's journals. That yellowing paper had inspired his report—the stupid report. Like a fool he'd been so excited to share it with his class, never dreaming the demon existed, never dreaming it could be summoned from across the ocean.

Matthew's grandparents had successfully escaped the monster and, that he knew of, his mother was never pursued by Abiku in America. But with the fresh image of Trent pacing and raving like a lunatic in his garage the morning before the millennium hit, Matthew didn't feel too sure anymore.

Never speak the horrid name again.

"Did I bring this on myself? Just by saying it out loud?" Matthew grabbed a pillow, put it over his face and crossed his arms over it, letting out a defeated groan.

For a few minutes he toyed with the idea of backing out of the trip proposed by Trent. What if he went to a movie or to the beach, and when Trent showed up to get him, he simply wasn't there? But that was unthinkable. *I have to be here. I have to face whatever fresh hell he's cooked up and stop him.*

"But how will I do that?" he muttered into the pillow. The prospect baffled him. Trent was so overwhelming, so intense, Matthew felt like a brittle leaf on a receding wave. Swept away, dragged into Trent's crazy world.

I let him, I wanted to be dragged, he thought. *No more though. Trent's not going to take me down with him.*

Matthew would either save Trent's life, or extinguish, once and for all, the last flame of hope. He wanted his friend to be superman again, but if it was not meant to be—then it wasn't. He flung the pillow across the living room.

He closed his eyes in a futile attempt to forget, or at least not to think about, what was going to happen that night.

CHAPTER SIX

Matthew fretted away the hours until four-thirty, choosing to leave the packing of his gear to the last minute.

He twirled his new goggles on his finger. The memory of a girl he'd met a couple of weeks ago while buying them came unbidden to his mind. What was her name?

Matthew had been at the Pro Shop when he ran into Amanda. He squirmed uncomfortably at the thought. Why did he have to be so awkward when it came to girls? Well, not all girls, just the ones he liked. He'd been able to talk to Amanda just fine; in fact, he thought of Amanda as another guy—she sure rode her bike like one. Matthew smirked. But Amanda's friend, what was her name? He remembered thinking not even Joan compared to Amanda's friend.

Matthew felt his face heat up with the same nervous, tongue-tying force of that day. *I'm such a loser*, he thought grimly, throwing the goggles on top of the unpacked gear bag.

Through the open front room windows, Matthew heard a diesel engine turn into the cul-de-sac. He stiffened as he peered out to the street and saw the tricked-up black Dodge Ram. One of the many ostentatious gifts Trent regularly received from his father, a man intent on making up with money for divorcing Trent's mother.

Matthew, like the other guys, knew all Trent had to do was voice his interest in something and bam! His father would flash an American Express, or cold hard cash, at the object of his son's desire. It had been a matter of days from Trent mentioning a motorcycle to when the Honda XR 400R, along with the trailer to haul it, showed up at his house.

Looking at the splendid bike even now gave Matthew a secret satisfaction, because he knew it had been he who'd gotten Trent started on his passion for off-road sports. *I gave him that*, Matthew thought ruefully.

The ease with which money was spent on Trent had dazed Matthew at first, so unlike the frugality practiced in his own home. But on this night, as Matthew watched Trent deftly back the trailer into his driveway, his wealth seemed all sour grapes. It's not envy, he told himself, it's that I know better now. "Wish I didn't," he muttered.

He grabbed his gear from the cabinet in the garage and threw it carelessly into the bag.

Nick and Kyle were already crammed in the back seat of the truck's dual cab. Chris scooted to the middle spot in the front bench seat. Judging by the loud welcome they gave him, Matthew didn't doubt they'd started the party without him. Trent wore a tired grin as he helped Matthew load his motorcycle in the trailer along with the other two bikes already tied down in it. The long bed of the truck carried two more.

Matthew wondered if the gray eyes behind the shades were bloodshot. Probably, or maybe, he thought unkindly, the pupils were contracted with that unseemly fear he'd glimpsed before.

They worked quickly and in silence. The exchanges between them were limited to a couple of glances and a "Thanks" on Matthew's part once his bike was secure and ready to go.

Matthew wedged the bag with his riding gear into a corner of the lined bed and climbed into the loud cab where the music rumbled, and the smell of tequila was pungent. Chris was the only other member of the crew who didn't enjoy the drug trips very much, but since it wasn't an option for any of them to stay clean or sober, Chris opted for hard liquor when circumstances called for it.

"Here you go, bro." Kyle tossed Matthew a cold beer from the cooler sandwiched between him and Nick in the back.

Matthew caught it and nodded in Kyle's direction.

"Pussy…" muttered Chris under his breath, then took a swig of tequila from his flask.

"Bite me," Matthew snapped back, sick of Chris' habit of conveying his opinions and bodily needs with as many obscenities as he could.

Chris gave him a loud, juicy-sounding, open-mouth burp.

Matthew frowned, torn between giving Chris a good elbow to the nose or going off on a tirade about tequila versus beer. Instead, Matthew turned away and looked out of the window. He took a couple of gulps from his beer.

Trent maneuvered them out of the neighborhood streets. They picked up speed as they headed out of Santee on Highway 67 toward the 8 Freeway, eastbound. The cab rattled with the deep bass of the stereo, as did Matthew's entire frame with the strained screeching of some unknown metal band blaring through the four speakers. The speedometer fluttered between eighty-five and a hundred. Matthew ran his fingers through his short hair and stared at the road ahead, much like Trent was doing; he drove with one hand on the steering wheel while in the other he held a beer.

The raucous good humor of the other three threw Matthew's and Trent's brooding attitudes into sharp relief.

Once off the freeway and on Highway 79, Trent seemed to regroup. He stopped looking so absorbed in his thoughts and started taking note of the truckload of people with him. With a good-humored smirk, he pulled over several times along the way for Chris to relieve himself.

"If you're gonna drink a can of beer for every shot," Trent said in his smart-ass tone of old, "you need to get a bladder enlargement, man." Everyone laughed, even Matthew.

Matthew's worries eased up a bit. He took a breather from the sinister aspect of their outing, which had been preying on him for months, and allowed himself a few boisterous laughs with the others. If only for the duration of the ride, Matthew slipped back to old times, when there used to be no clouds in their skies. When all was fun and games and their disputes were resolved through displays of the most aromatic, loud or just plain disgusting bodily emissions. That Trent had hinted to the preparations he'd made, that it sounded as if Trent had read his grandmother's secret pages and was preparing to carry out the ancient ritual Abiku demanded of his priests, seemed to Matthew a foolish fear, so far-fetched it was embarrassing to even consider it could happen.

Yet they were on their way.

As Matthew and Trent once again rolled down the windows to air out the cab from Chris' latest "insult" amid curses and appreciative laughter, Matthew found himself longing for the past. He wished he could turn back the clock. He would be firm with Trent about the drugs. He himself wouldn't try them, not even once. And NO, he wouldn't indulge Trent; he would say exactly what he thought and felt because after all, Trent *did* listen to him, or he used to anyway. *Now he only listens to himself,* he thought bitterly. *Or to Abiku.*

Matthew shook his head, spooked. He eyed Trent with suspicion and alarm, but Trent was banging his head to the beat of the music coming out of the speakers, as were Chris, Kyle and Nick—nothing fearsome or suspicious about that.

When they got to Warner Springs, they took the S22 turnoff to Anza Borrego State Park. The winding, mountainous road they'd been on opened to a wide and rippled road that cut through the desert. They followed it to the campsite Trent had chosen, south of Ocotillo Wells, a couple of miles off the paved road.

No sooner had Trent parked the truck and trailer than the passengers stumbled out of the cab to stretch their limbs and stare at the serene desert, a sight that never failed to take Matthew's breath away.

The sun was low in the western horizon as they began to unload their bikes, quickly and efficiently, all the while heckling Chris about his drunken remarks.

They shed their suburban clothing and for a few minutes they were bare-chested, bare-legged boys, in nothing but boxer briefs, digging through their gear bags or chasing each other around the truck and trailer. Trent kept them on task though.

The gear they'd flung at each other was recovered, item by item, and soon they all donned the required armor. Just like that, they'd morphed into warlike apparitions.

They wore full-face helmets and goggles. Their chest protectors looked like synthetic rib cages over their long-sleeve jerseys. They wore leather, poly-grip gloves fastened to their wrists with Velcro strips. Their nylon riding pants had cupped knees and sufficient padding to withstand road rash should they be dragged on the dirt by their bikes. To complete the look, they wore heavy steel-toed leather boots, despite which they walked easily around the campsite, filling up their tanks and stowing their bags in the cab, as if not an ounce of their armor was felt.

They started and revved their engines. For a moment, the air around them was clouded with exhaust fumes and dust from Chris making donuts on the dirt.

Trent signaled and, as one, they took off abruptly, like a pack of wolves trailing a scent.

Five funnels of dust settled. The truck and trailer sat forlorn in the silent campsite.

* * * *

The heat rising from the ground gave the red horizon a watery look that made Matthew think of mirages, and of the ancient *Kung Fu* episodes his grandfather loved to watch. Looking behind him one last time, he saw the last sliver of sun disappear. He fought off the overwhelming sensation that the darkness he was headed toward was more than just night.

Trent took the lead and the remainder of the squadron paired up behind him.

They rampaged through the barren desert, their thrill enhanced by LSD and tequila. All except for Matthew who only had one beer and, as usual, was content with the rush he got from the speed and power of his motorcycle. On this night, he looked forward to the blinding force to soothe and release his tension. He cranked the throttle and lost himself in the deafening roar of the bike until his mind quieted.

Inside his helmet, the sounds of the wind and the guttural responses of his body to the rough ride obliterated his worries. Through his dusty goggles his eyes devoured the terrain rushing at him, and his brain surveyed and measured furiously in the microseconds he had to anticipate his trajectory. Trent was in front of him and Matthew kept to the right of him, out of his dust.

The sky grew darker to the east. The glow of twilight receded, and all Matthew could see was what appeared before him in the narrow cone of his headlight.

Bike and rider shook so much it was almost impossible to see where he would land next, but that uncertainty was exactly what drove him. Matthew couldn't ease up on the throttle, and he could hear himself groaning and cussing. The fear of not knowing made his stomach turn, but what a rush! To lift off the ground unexpectedly, with only a fraction of a second to prepare for the inevitable jolt of landing, and in the next instant, with his insides still quaking, be forced to react again to whatever the desert put in his way.

The warning thoughts that had plagued him became too dim to demand an actual resolution, but they were still there, like annoying little gnats. Thoughts about Trent, thoughts about the reason his grandparents left Africa, thoughts about the fateful history report that brought them here on this night. *How was I supposed to know?* he thought defensively, but he also wondered, how can those idiots stay on their bikes?

Matthew's senses were intact and still, every second was an excruciating effort to keep up with Trent at 60 mph. Hell, a 250 is no match for an XR 400R, he thought. But the others were loaded, yet they rode all over the place at incredible speed without any apparent balance handicaps. He could hear their howling noises and curses of sheer exhilaration and Matthew smiled to himself, knowing exactly why they could stay upright on their bikes. *They're wasted.*

Matthew lost sight of Trent in the dust. He swung further to the right again and got in the clear. There was Trent, about twenty yards ahead. He kept pace on his 250 and it occurred to Matthew, out of the blue, that Trent, on his powerful 400R, was pulling him like some bizarre magnet. His smile faded beneath his helmet. The idea bothered him; did he really have no choice, no control? From somewhere in his imagination, his grandmother shook her head, and something inside Matthew wavered. He gunned his 250, to break the pace as much as to dispel the creepy sense that Trent was dragging him someplace from which he'd never be able to return.

"What the hell am I doing out here..." he muttered in the contained world filled with sounds inside his helmet.

Matthew's body continued to do its job mechanically, in direct response to the messages sent by his brain. He leaned into a jump, twisting his handlebar to the right while up in the air. He flicked his tongue over his teeth, tasting the dust in his mouth. He clenched his jaw to avoid biting his tongue when he hit the ground. "Damn!" He grunted, fumbling for the foot-peg and not finding it. He squeezed the bike with his thighs, they already quaked from the strain; he tried to get his bearings, his right hand at full throttle. Matthew hit the ground awkwardly with his weight almost entirely on his left leg, but he didn't topple.

When he got things under control, Matthew noticed Trent had slowed down and was scanning a not-so-distant point on the horizon.

The constant rumble of the engine vibrated through him, making him feel like his arms and his crotch were crawling with ants. He'd been so tense his forearms and hands ached as if he'd been riding for hours.

"Yeehaw!" Chris' hokey war cry reached Matthew. He knew the other three were high with anticipation because Trent had worked them up with the idea of an initiation. They were there along for the ride, along with whatever Trent decided.

A wave of disgust rose inside of him and Matthew undid the strap of his helmet. He lifted it enough to spit out the unexpected bitter taste that had come to his mouth.

I will talk to my parents about Trent. That's what I need to do. Trent is definitely out of my control, and if I'm going to help him, I'll need help myself, Matthew thought, and this simple and suddenly obvious decision made a huge difference—there might still be a positive outcome. He trusted that in time, and with proper medical or psychological attention, Trent might once again be that guy he'd met a year before, sound and full of promise.

Matthew and the others stopped to watch their leader as he studied a campsite a quarter of a mile away, distinguishable only because of the bulk of two motor homes. He seemed to be keeping a good hundred feet between himself and the site. Matthew didn't even want to think what was going through Trent's mind.

"Where the fuck are we?" Chris wanted to know as he stumbled around relieving himself.

Kyle made a crude remark about Chris' bladder as Trent pulled up beside Matthew. *I'm his second,* Matthew thought. *Those little gestures of Trent's never failed to flatter him, but if I'm gonna help him, I need to be number one now.*

He followed Trent's gaze toward the peaceful campsite. The motor homes were parked at an angle and between them, two men were building a fire.

Matthew knew how the camping routine went and the familiarity of it made him homesick for his father and the rest of his family, even Samantha, with her wisecracks and all. *How right she was about Trent,* he couldn't help thinking.

The two men were piling wood, in that slow, comfortable way Matthew knew came from sore limbs, tired of riding, and no doubt from a couple of beers at the end of the day, just to take the edge off the aches. It made for easy conversation while readying for a night of joking and laughing by the fire, under the immense desert sky. Matthew's family on his father's side were a clan of seasoned campers. Yes, he knew how that went.

"It's show-time, girls!" Trent announced in a fiery voice, and in contrast with his earlier mood he now seemed awake and energized.

Matthew's memories of laid-back camping trips from an innocent lifetime ago recoiled at the sound of Trent's devilish voice. The reality of the moment struck him again. He shuddered and heard himself breathing heavily inside his helmet.

Matthew spotted a slow-moving headlight. It was a quad-runner, leaving the campsite and venturing out into the darkened desert. The quad plugged along up the slope. *Amateur rider*, he thought to himself but remembered fondly when he too was just learning the ins and outs of the sport. How grown up he'd felt when his father at last let him ride by himself and venture out a couple of miles from camp. The code of the desert was that big riders helped the little ones. It was safe. His eyes shifted toward Trent and he cringed beneath his armor when he found Trent staring at him, scrutinizing him.

Matthew looked away and focused on the quad, thankful for the full-face helmet. An unnatural chill seeped into him through his jersey and Matthew instinctively feared for the rider on that quad. The code would be broken.

CHAPTER SEVEN

"Justin, aren't you done yet?" twelve-year-old Mary called, feeling very tough as she leaned against the quad-runner she had finally been allowed to ride by herself.

"I'm almost done!" the tiny voice replied.

"I hate these outhouses!" she muttered.

Justin stumbled out, fixing his pants and T-shirt.

"Are you sure you didn't touch anything in there?" she said, her lip curling with disgust at the thought of her little brother touching the filthy mockery of a toilet inside.

"I tried not to, but I had to hold on to something or I'd fall in!" he defended himself.

"Well, that's why you should've let me go in and help you," she nagged, but smiled at him while she tucked his shirt in for him.

Mary helped Justin with his helmet and then sat him on the quad while she put her own helmet and gloves on. They started back to camp.

"I'm all grown up now and Mom says I need my privacy!" Justin remembered to add, raising his voice so Mary could hear him over the sound of the engine.

Mary laughed out loud, squeezing the little hands holding tight to her waist. She felt all grown up herself and she rode with great caution, feeling responsible for her five-year-old brother. It was her intent not to tamper with the trust her parents had placed in her. She figured she would have plenty of opportunities later in the weekend to ride on her own and be able to do it faster. Of course, she'd have to take turns with her nine-year-old sister, who was still learning, but for tonight, Mary was excited enough that they had let her ride around camp. And then, bonus! The daring, though she did realize it, unnecessary half-mile trip to the outhouse, since both of the two motor homes were equipped with toilets.

Justin's helmet kept banging on her back. She remembered being smaller herself and trying so hard not to bang her dad's back when he took her for rides. Her dad had told her it was important to hold her head steady, so it didn't whip around when they rode rougher. So, she passed the advice on to her brother and he said, "Okay." His head thumped her back.

Mary could hear the *wing-din-din* racket of motorcycle engines over the sound of the quad, and she looked to see where they were coming from. At her right, she counted five headlights racing downhill not too far from her, and she secretly wished she were big enough to ride a real bike like they did. She loved the way boys looked in thick riding pants and leather boots, and the chest protectors and helmets with all the flashy designs. Yes, they had to be good-looking boys.

The five riders were closing in and though Mary was sure they could see her, because she had her orange flag and her headlight was on, she feared they might come too close and run her off the trail, so she accelerated to get out of their path.

"I know you're all grown up," Mary said smiling. "You're so grown up, that one of these days you won't even need ME to take you to the bathroom!" she teased.

Justin gave her waist a squeeze and she knew he was smiling underneath his helmet.

"We're almost to the top of this hill," Mary announced, glancing quickly at her brother and at the bikes coming after them. But Mary counted only three bikes now instead of the original five.

"Go over the slope really fast so my belly tickles, okay?" Justin urged.

"Yeah, sure... But remember to—"

Her words were cut short by the blaring noise of larger engines. She looked toward the top of the slope, startled to see the two missing motorcycles materialize in the air in front of her. They flew off the summit and she screamed in panic. They were going to land on her and Justin.

The other three bikes kept coming from behind but were still a way off. She felt the earth tremble when the two bikes hit the ground only a couple of feet in front of her. She swerved to the left, leaning into the turn like her father had taught her, and hoping Justin would be strong enough to hold on. He was. She managed to avoid crashing into the first bike that skidded to a halt in front of her, but she was blinded by the dust and so frightened by the loud engines she lost control of the quad.

Justin held fast to her waist, that being her only comfort when they both rushed to the ground despite her efforts to stay on the quad. Mary scrambled in the dirt and tried frantically to pull her brother closer to her, but a strong arm snatched Justin from behind her. The back tire of the bike slid then caught. Mary shielded her face against the spray of dirt that issued from it like a rooster tail as the bike sped away.

"Rough her up a bit," Mary heard him yell to the others. There seemed to be so many, but she remembered she'd counted only five. "It'll buy us some time and then you know where to meet me."

Time for what? Mary wondered. The dust cleared long enough for her to see the rider's arm braced under Justin's armpit and across his little chest, but in the next moment, Justin was swiftly draped across the rider's lap and spirited away on the huge bike. A second rider took off after them.

They left Mary behind with nothing but the lingering feeling of Justin's small arms around her waist and the echoing sound of the panic-stricken squeal he let out as they raced away. Mary was now in the uncertain company of the three other riders who'd arrived in a whirl of sound, dust and exhaust fumes. They circled her fiercely, accelerating jerkily, taunting her.

"Please don't hurt him!" she heard herself plead pathetically, shielding her eyes from the clouds of dust raised by their tires.

"Hurt who?" one of them laughed. "Matt? He loves Matt." They all jeered and laughed.

They didn't see him, Mary thought. There was so much dust... They didn't even see Justin.

She didn't think they'd help Justin even if they knew the rider on the large bike had taken him.

Mary thrashed on the dirt, trying to avoid their tires. She knew by their slurred speech and the detached hostility in their tone that they were drunk or high on something. The brutal sense of the situation wiped away her instinct to act, but a high-pitched gasp escaped her when one of them landed a kick on her helmeted head. The sudden reality of her predicament soaked every quivering cell in her body. One of them ripped her helmet off. A boot connected with her unprotected head. A spray of stars blinded her.

Completely vulnerable to their blows now, Mary wilted on the ground like a ragdoll. They began beating her and did not stop until she was dead, or at least appeared to be.

Mary could hear them laughing and she sought comfort in the thought that at least she had the rest of her gear on, though for all she knew, they were not finished with her. Her skin felt as thick as gums injected with Novocain. She couldn't feel the pain anymore. Mary saw the full moon low in the sky through what she knew must be blood, coming down her forehead and into her eyes. Mary lay still. Her mind raced.

* * * *

The three stopped to survey the scene.

"It's dead," Chris announced crudely, still dazed by hallucinations.

"Jesus! You're the crassest!" Nick complained in disgust. He had restrained himself when he saw the helmet come off the girl's head. "Let's just get out of here..."

And with that, they took off in the direction they'd seen Trent and Matthew go.

* * * *

It's dead... It's dead... They mean me!

Mary uttered a painful moan that died at the top of her throat. A primitive instinct told her they must have crushed every bone in her body, though the pain didn't seem to register in her mind. Justin...

Her campsite was less than a mile away, just over the slope, and though it seemed like an eternity, she knew the attack had been swift and it would be another twenty minutes before her parents started looking for her.

Mary could not feel her lips, nor could she find in her brain the coordinating ability to utter a cry for help. Terror boiled inside of her.

Daddy—

CHAPTER EIGHT

Half a dozen flashlights cut through the darkness in frantic search.

The desperate cries of a woman slashed through the night, "Oh my God! My God!"

"Over this way!" Mary's father alerted the search party. He cleared his throat, so his voice wouldn't break again. His wife's blood-curdling scream had gone into him like the cold shaft of a dagger. "I think she found something!"

"Good God almighty!" he gasped.

He looked at the gruesome scene, feeling nothing like himself, as if this couldn't be happening to him. Yet it was. His wife's shoulders shook beneath his hands and he couldn't stop her. Didn't think he should. A knot like a bowling ball was stuck at the top of his throat and he spit, because he couldn't swallow at this point. He looked at his wife again, hunched over the body of a young girl who had been beautiful once, so full of hope. Now she lay curled in a heap before them, brutally beaten and hardly a shadow of her former self.

The crying stopped quite suddenly, and his wife's horror-stricken face looked away from their broken daughter. She howled in desperation, her bulging eyes fixed on him, "Where is Justin?!"

He gripped her shoulders in sheer helplessness and drew her up from the ground where she'd been kneeling by Mary. He held her in his arms, hoping to console her—and himself in the process. Most of all, he wanted to vent the rage he felt as he looked again at his sweet Mary.

CHAPTER NINE

"So, you don't think your friend Matthew will be there?" Sophie asked Amanda. She tried to sound casual about it but the faint blush creeping to her cheeks gave her away. She slung her duffel bag from her shoulder and dropped it on the floor of the garage.

"Probably not," Amanda replied with a knowing smirk. "The season's pretty much over and this is an out-of-the-blue trip—mostly so you don't have to see the place crawling with rowdy bikers," she said, surveying the contents of her bag with her hands on her hips. "Lucky school's closed, huh?" she added, nestling her helmet among the riding pants, jersey and gloves already packed.

"Yeah, lucky the pipes blew in the lunchroom and lucky your parents are such good sports," said Sophie. "Oh well," she sighed with a smile to hide her disappointment. She'd only seen Matthew once a few weeks back, but she kept hoping to run into him again.

* * * *

Amanda had moved to Carlsbad at the beginning of the school year and the two girls had been drawn to each other with the pull of opposites attracting. Since their friendship began, Amanda had done nothing but rave about her sport of choice, motocross, and about the feeling of power she got from having a machine so powerful at her command. She talked about rushing down Blow Sand hill (a landmark Amanda promised to show Sophie upon arrival at their destination), feeling almost vertical, and the impending sensation she could fly off her bike at any moment.

"It's such a charge!" Amanda claimed the high-gear shuddering of the engine rattled every inch of her, giving her a thrill that couldn't compare to anything she had ever experienced.

Sophie, being more on the romantic side, was doubtful though willing and eager to be persuaded. And now that the moment was at hand, Amanda's contagious excitement threatened to overwhelm her.

Over the preceding months, Sophie, with her subdued and ladylike demeanor, was in a state of constant agitation over Amanda's boisterous behavior. Amanda had an uncontrollable urge to communicate every thought and feeling as soon as they popped into her mind.

Sophie, on the other hand, took the pensive approach and tried her best to think before she spoke. Sophie's thoughtfulness toward others contrasted sharply with Amanda's self-centered slant. The fact Sophie had an extrasensory ability that often allowed her exceptionally accurate peeps into other people's thoughts only added to her considerate nature, whereas Amanda blundered around, oblivious to the feelings of others. Amanda called this ability Sophie's "witchy side," or when in a less generous mood and looking to antagonize, her parlor trick.

But their differences didn't stop at personalities. Their physical attributes were also at opposite ends of the spectrum.

Sophie had dark red hair and almond-shaped eyes in a Caribbean shade of green. She was five feet four inches tall and had more of a Greek nose to go with her full lips. Her Irish-Polynesian ancestry gave her an exotic air, which was accentuated by her reserved nature.

Amanda was a brunette with sparkly brown eyes who laughed at everything. Sophie often told her that if it weren't for Amanda's towering height of almost six feet, she would be the embodiment of a pixie, with a tiny button nose and all.

"Wish I could compliment you like that," Amanda had retorted briskly one day. "But when I look at you, all I can think of is some stiff British lady from the eighteen hundreds."

"I consider myself totally complimented," Sophie replied with a satisfied grin.

The girls understood and loved one another unconditionally. And aside from Sophie's parents, Amanda was the only person who knew about Sophie's witchy side.

* * * *

The Hinckleys' 28-foot motor home had a trailer hitched to it, overloaded with camping supplies plus the brand new, neon-green sand rail they had added to their collection of toys—and of course, Amanda's Honda 250, her baby, her love.

They were all inside the roomy motor home now, waiting for Mr. Hinckley.

Sophie was more than infected with Amanda's excitement; she literally had a stomachache and wanted nothing more than to start moving. As Sophie saw it, the only drawback to this trip was Oliver, Amanda's twelve-year-old brother, who had a crush on her and who seemed determined to gawk at her the entire trip. He had positioned himself across from Sophie and Amanda in the dining area, appearing positively star-struck. Sophie admitted to herself that, even though it was just Oliver, it was still flattering.

Sophie gave him a secret but direct smile that completely leveled him. His face got so blotchy with embarrassment she almost giggled but refrained, not wanting to embarrass him further.

Mr. Hinckley finally came in and took the driver's seat. He grumbled something about needing to buy a new garage-door opener, and on that note, they finally took off.

As the large vehicle made its way out of town, Amanda talked nonstop about the wonders of the desert and explained to Sophie, in detail, the mechanics of riding a bike until Sophie was dizzy with information.

The Hinckleys normally camped at Ocotillo Wells in Anza Borrego Park, but this time they were going further south, closer to the Salton Sea, where they were sure to find dunes and the type of terrain more suitable for the sand rail. They were looking forward to trying out their new toy.

Larry and Kristen Hinckley had an easy way about them that made Sophie smile. She felt right at home with them. Mr. Hinckley insisted on stretching his legs every so often and Mrs. Hinckley seemed to remember last-minute things every five miles, causing them to stop at every food mart they happened by. Amanda was fit to be tied over all the delays.

Sophie sighed, amused by their squabbles, while Oliver kept to himself in his seat across from her. She knew he was on the lookout for her next smile.

They had been late in leaving, and the two-and-a-half-hour trip ended up being almost four hours with all the rest and shopping stops. It was almost eleven o'clock that night when they found what seemed like a good place to set up camp.

The previous campers had made a circle of stones for a fire pit, a very elaborate one consisting of three concentric rings. In it, Mr. Hinckley and Oliver dumped a third of the firewood they had brought along. Everyone was tired and even Amanda decided to abandon her plan to ride upon arrival, no matter how late. At that point, she just wanted to "sleep because the sooner I do, the sooner it'll be morning."

Mrs. Hinckley helped turn the dining room into a bed for Sophie and Amanda and it was a cozy little sleeping place. In a matter of minutes, they were all ready for bed.

Outside, the breeze blew gently, and a myriad of twinkling eyes punctured the sky.

CHAPTER TEN

Amanda arose with the sun. The huffing and puffing as she put on her gear woke Sophie within minutes.

"You look like a power ranger," Sophie mumbled through a yawn. She hadn't slept very well, and her eyes felt grainy. She rubbed them, thinking she didn't like the cramped quarters and the proximity of so many other people. The eerie silence of the desert and the collection of noises the Hinckleys made had created an alien atmosphere she couldn't relax in.

The bathroom was a problem for Sophie. She couldn't get used to the tiny compartment housing a toilet, sink and a small shower. She made a mental note to use it preferably when the motor home was empty. She didn't want anyone to hear her bodily functions and hygiene rituals as she'd heard Mr. Hinckley's the night before.

"And you look like *Night of the Living Dead*," was Amanda's response, as she pulled her heavy boots almost up to her knees and ran the Velcro strips through the metal fasteners up the sides.

Sophie sat up smiling, resolved to make the best of all of it. "Good morning to you too," she said, getting up and hurrying to turn the bed back into a dining room before breakfast.

"Good morning, girls!" Mrs. Hinckley said, sliding open the accordion-like door that separated their compartment from the rest of the motor home. "You're so swift, Sophie, thank you for taking care of the bed for me." She moved easily about the compact kitchen, warming up sausage and preparing toaster strudels and waffles for everyone while Mr. Hinckley, who got up shortly after her, started a pot of coffee.

Oliver gawked at Sophie from his bed above the cab, but he snapped out of his reverie when Sophie looked straight at him, daring him to say or do something, which of course, he didn't.

"I slept like a log," Mrs. Hinckley commented. "I tell you, I completely over-exerted myself planning this trip on such short notice and now I'm so exhausted I won't be able to do anything but sleep the next two days."

"Oh, but you won't!" Mr. Hinckley answered, standing behind his wife and squeezing her shoulders. "We have a new toy to play with, remember?"

"Oh yeah…that!" Mrs. Hinckley smiled.

"Mom! Is it ready yet?" Amanda grumbled. She was sitting at the table in full riding gear, drumming her fingers.

"In a minute," Mrs. Hinckley said, frustrated with the paper plates that were stuck together.

"Here, I'll do that," her husband offered, and she winked at him, moving on to setting the milk and syrup on the table while Amanda and Sophie got the napkins and plastic utensils.

"Sophie, did you sleep okay?" Mrs. Hinckley wanted to know. She handed Amanda her plate with a blueberry strudel and three sausage links.

"Yes, thank you," Sophie replied. "I'm so excited about today!"

"We brought an extra helmet and goggles for you," Amanda said with a mouthful of sausage as she squeezed icing from a plastic pouch onto her pastry.

"Don't talk with your mouth full, please," Mr. Hinckley frowned. "Oliver, will you get the coffee cups from that cabinet up there?"

Rather than coming down from his bunk, Oliver reached over lazily to open the cabinet. All its contents spilled on Sophie's head because they had shifted during the trip. With a yelp, Sophie glanced up at him and could tell from his pained expression that the whole suave maneuver he'd been hoping for had backfired. He turned beet-red as he climbed down, humiliated, to clean up the mess.

Amanda let out a pitiless laugh, which fizzled out under Sophie's he's-embarrassed-enough-as-it-is frown. Amanda bit into her last piece of sausage.

"It's okay. Grab those over there," Sophie smiled kindly at Oliver, pointing to the plastic cups strewn on the floor.

She helped Oliver pack everything back in the cabinet before they ate their breakfast. Mr. and Mrs. Hinckley had coffee and cereal due to their new diet, and as soon as they were all finished, they took turns in the bathroom. Eventually, Mr. Hinckley and Oliver went out to gas up the toys for the day. Amanda and her mom, in a display of thoughtful consideration, went to test the awning, and Sophie got the last turn; the compartment was all hers and nobody would hear her.

* * * *

Sophie stepped out of the motor home ready for the day and was awestruck by what she saw. It was eight o'clock in the morning and the sky was a crisp blue, so different from Carlsbad's hazy, coastal sky. It reminded her of a vacation she and her parents had spent in Breckenridge, Colorado. There too she had seen a sky that blue and that clear. She remembered thinking maybe it had something to do with the cold and altitude, but now she knew it didn't.

The rugged mountains, like mammoth stacks of rocks, seemed to be pasted flat to the horizon. She knew they were three-dimensional, had to be, but she wondered anyway. She shook her head staring at the far-off hills—cardboard thin against the blue background. So intense was the illusion Sophie thought it a miracle.

Sophie left the shade of the awning and stepped into the bright sunlight. The warmth of the early sun struck her as a serious warning of the heat to come later in the day.

It was almost the end of May and it seemed they were the only campers there. Too late for spring, everyone would of course skip summer on account of the heat, and too early for fall; the desert was all theirs. Sophie let out a sigh as she looked beyond their campsite, not a hint of any other camping parties. "Amanda *did* say he wouldn't be here," she said to herself, thinking about Matthew and realizing again just how much she'd been wishing to see him again and maybe talk to him. The pipes at his school probably haven't busted, she told herself.

Their day was spent in a series of excursions, Amanda and Oliver on their bikes, while Sophie rode with Mr. & Mrs. Hinckley in the back of their four-seater sand rail.

For miles around, it seemed, Sophie could see nothing but mounds of cream-colored sand in varying heights. Mr. and Mrs. Hinckley took turns driving the buggy, and Sophie agreed to try it when they offered. But the sand rail stalled halfway up a dune and then slid sideways on her first attempt. She thought for sure they would roll, but the buggy proved to be very stable.

"The gearshift takes some getting used to," Mr. Hinckley told her, and Sophie gave him a shaky nod. "You'll try it again when we're on flat ground, like the wash we rode on to get here," he suggested.

"That sounds great," Sophie replied, thinking it *would* be a lot easier to fumble with a clutch on wide-open terrain.

On their way back to camp, Mr. Hinckley guided them into a maze of miniature canyons for a nerve-wracking tour. Sophie grinned in the back seat of the buggy, her head whipped around to catch glimpses of Amanda and Oliver weaving and sliding between the reddish walls that lined the narrow pathways. She amused herself pretending they were gigantic Transformers playing in the Grand Canyon.

After a light lunch back at camp, they took a long ride to the rank shores of the Salton Sea. As they ripped along, Sophie heard Mr. Hinckley say, "Every year it gets smaller."

Mrs. Hinckley shook her head. "Global warming and evaporation," she replied.

Sadder than that, thought Sophie, was that in the heat of the desert, the smell of the shrinking lake was like raw sewage.

But Sophie had to admit, once she got past the stench, the lake was a rather beautiful sight.

Not until five that afternoon, when the sun began its descent, did they start back to camp. Sophie climbed out of the buggy crusted over with sweat and dust, and sore from being jostled, even though she'd been safely strapped in the whole time.

"I wonder if sand can be considered fiber," Mrs. Hinckley joked, as she stamped her boots and shook the dust off herself before stepping on the fake grass pad they'd placed under the awning.

Mr. Hinckley and Oliver took out the hamburgers and hot dogs to be grilled for dinner while the girls went into the motor home to clean themselves up.

Amanda sat on the toilet and talked to Sophie in her characteristically animated way and they laughed, remembering some of the stunts she had pulled that day. Sophie washed her face in the kitchen sink and tried to fix her braid so that it looked somewhat decent after wearing a helmet all day. Her head felt oddly weightless and she was exhausted but completely thrilled with the new experiences the day had brought.

Though she hadn't said anything to Amanda, Sophie had made up her mind to give the bike a try. It looked like so much more fun than the sand rail, or at least Amanda made it seem that way. She rode with such ease Sophie was certain she would be able to do it too. Her mind was filled with images of her skinny best friend, flying down Blow Sand hill or tearing through the rough terrain, fearless and free. Soaring above the ground and landing without so much as a thump, only to race ahead into that unreachable horizon, with nothing in her way.

"Sophie, would you take these rocks out please?" Mrs. Hinckley said, tripping over a pile of them on her way to the kitchen. "I don't know why Oliver insists on piling up this junk!"

"Sure, Mrs. Hinckley," Sophie said, and added on Oliver's behalf, "he mentioned something about looking for fossils on them…or something like that."

"Well, throw them in the back of the trailer then. That way they're out of my way and he won't be upset we lost them."

Remembering the fancy fire pit built by the previous campers, Sophie scooped up the pretty round stones Oliver had collected and headed outside with them.

"Oliver!" she called, "I'm going to—" She pushed open the screen door of the motor home with her foot, awkwardly holding the half dozen stones to her chest as she stepped down, "—put these in…" She couldn't finish her sentence. The screen slamming shut behind her was the last normal thing she heard.

A faint lamentation filled the air around Sophie. She stopped, disoriented—the stones became heavier in her hands, spreading an odd chill to her solar plexus. Her glance roved over the familiar campsite, registering nothing. Her throat tightened, wondering for a moment if the deeply heartbreaking lament was coming from her own soul! The weeping possessed her, a sweltering fear infected her, and she stiffened as her blood seemed to drain to her feet. Sophie wobbled a little.

In a daze, she saw Oliver coming toward her. *Good*, she thought, *he can take these.* From miles away, it seemed, Mr. Hinckley arranged kindling for that night's fire—the pit wasn't more than fifteen feet away.

"Are you bringing the buns?" Oliver winked in a trivial attempt to charm her.

His voice reached her several seconds after she'd seen his lips form the words, and from the midst of her stupor, she sputtered, "Um… What? Yes—I mean NO! Here you go." She dumped the half dozen stones into his outstretched hands. "Your mom wants them in the trailer, out of the way."

What the hell was that, she wondered, startled out of her wits.

"Are you all right?" Oliver said, a concerned frown on his face. "You look kinda pale."

"Do I?" Sophie said, putting her hands over her cheeks. "Yeah, sure, I'm fine—" She gave him a nervous smile then returned to the motor home, feeling shaky and confused.

The screen door slammed shut behind her and the chill she'd felt began to thaw in the warm kitchen.

"Thank you, sweetie," Mrs. Hinckley smiled.

"Mmm, welcome," Sophie murmured, casting about for reassurances that whatever had taken her over was gone.

The sound of the toilet flushing came from further inside the motor home. Amanda came out zipping up her riding pants. "S'up?"

Sophie exhaled.

* * * *

That night, they sat around the fire on folding chairs and prepared to eat the sumptuous dinner Mr. Hinckley and Oliver had prepared. Sophie tried to sidestep her thoughts, wanting to believe she had imagined the whole thing, but the intense sense of grief washed over her anew, making it impossible for her not to think about it.

"I never knew a dune buggy could be so much fun," she heard herself say, determined to override it at least while others were around her. "Though I think I have eaten enough dirt to give those watermelon seeds I ate a fine bed to sprout from."

They all laughed, and Sophie slowly let herself relax and join in the ensuing conversation as a way of fully dispelling her demons. They shared different versions of the thrills they experienced that day, and they laughed until Sophie had almost put the eerie incident out of her mind.

"What's the deal with those rocks?" Amanda asked.

Sophie tensed, realizing that at some point during dinner, Oliver must have retrieved two of them from the trailer, as he was now handling them.

"They have gold in them!" Oliver explained, juggling them from one hand to the other.

"I thought you were looking for fossils," Sophie confronted him, and Oliver shook his head.

"Oh bull! Fool's gold for sure!" Amanda laughed. "They look like runty ostrich eggs."

"Let me see," Mr. Hinckley said. "I'll tell you if they have gold in them or not." He began a thorough inspection to humor his son. "I'm no geologist, but I'm afraid they won't make a millionaire out of you," he concluded after a full forty seconds. He handed them to his wife saying, "But they are quite nice to look at, *and* we could use them for our pond in the back yard."

"Now there's an idea," she said, admiring the almost artificial finish of the smooth white surfaces.

The stones circulated among them and they all commented on how beautiful they were. Amanda grinned and passed one to Sophie, rolling her eyes as she did so. As soon as Sophie touched it, the sound came again. She hastily put it down, realizing directly what the source of her experience had been. Her heart pounded in her chest as she looked at Amanda and her family, but it seemed they hadn't noticed her reaction at all. Sophie took a deep breath to calm herself while glancing suspiciously at the stone she'd dropped on the ground.

Oliver picked it up with a hopeful glance at her, and Sophie smiled nervously.

* * * *

Amanda had promised they'd sleep outside, and although fearful, Sophie couldn't wait for the others to leave her and Amanda alone. She wanted to find out what came next.

CHAPTER ELEVEN

Mr. and Mrs. Hinckley went to bed, taking Oliver with them, but Sophie and Amanda sat by the fire making small talk until Sophie worked up the nerve to tell her friend what had happened. She described to Amanda what she'd heard as soon as she touched the rocks and how it had made her feel.

Sophie sat back and let the revelation sink in. In the cool night air, she watched Amanda watch the fire. Just when she thought she should say something to hurry her friend along, she looked up.

"So, what's the deal? Why don't you just grab one of them and get it over with?" Amanda said, picking up one of the stones and bouncing it on her palm. "Blows my mind that you can see so much with just a touch while I can't even get a tingle out of it. You're not making this up, are you?" Amanda looked at Sophie with a raised brow.

"I wish I were," Sophie admitted. Her lip quivered but she bit down on it. "I'm scared, Amanda, this was different—way stronger than other stuff before."

"Oh, just do it, c'mon. Here!" she said, offering the stone to Sophie.

Sophie took it. She wrapped her fingers around its smooth surface, making a fist over it. Her palm sealed against it.

"Well? Tell me what you see!"

"There's a little boy—" Sophie answered, trying to swallow the big knot that formed in her throat the second she had touched it, as if she'd become the boy! "He's very weak and very scared. There's this guy—he's big. And the boy, his neck—his little neck feels wet and sticky."

"You're not making any sense. Who's the big guy?"

Sophie almost didn't hear her. Amanda's questions seemed to reach her from across a vast field. "He has gray eyes—the guy. He's so rough on the little boy," Sophie said blankly.

"Why—what does the boy look like?"

"I can't see the boy. But the big guy's eyes look like the rocks in the desert," Sophie whispered. She *was* the little boy. "Can't see the stars for the fire—but *my* neck, it's sticky," she murmured, and a distant bell chimed, signaling that she should separate herself from the vision, for her own sake as much as her friend's. "*He's* falling asleep, but he doesn't want to—"

"Is he bleeding, Sofe?" Amanda pleaded. "If he's bleeding, he shouldn't fall asleep."

Sophie's intense concentration kept her rocking back and forth in her chair, completely unaware of it. "My eyes—I mean, his eyes are closing!"

Amanda rocked with her. "Is he dead? Sofe?"

Sophie let the stone roll out of her hand onto the ground, her heart fluttering in her chest like a caged bird. "I can't see anything anymore."

Although the vision had dissipated along with the sense of terror, the gray eyes with the stony expression glinted in Sophie's brain as if they meant to watch her from within. Becoming aware of the cool night air penetrating her clothes and her flesh, she looked over at Amanda, and managed an awkward grin as she drew her knees to her chest and wrapped her arms around them.

Rubbing Sophie from shoulder to elbow, and with a fretful scowl plastered on her face, Amanda said, "Tell me again what you saw—I couldn't get a bunch of what you said."

"Was I rambling on?" Sophie leaned away from Amanda's frantic rub-down.

The friction ceased. "You said all kinds of stuff that sounded out of sequence."

"Um," Sophie tried to sort out her thoughts; everything seemed to progress from A to B quite logically while she was seeing it, much in the same way dreams make sense while one is in them. She shuddered. "It's so weird, even though I'm not holding the stone anymore, I can still feel—"

"You can still feel what?" Amanda inched closer and squeezed Sophie's arm.

"The guilt. *Not supposed to go with strangers,*" Sophie whispered, and tears sprang from her eyes, remembering the terror the little boy had experienced. The thought of him enduring it, all alone, suddenly angered her. "I wish I could tell him he *didn't go*, he was taken! He would *never* be in trouble with his momma for such a thing! That is what he was so worried about, that his mom was going to be upset with him!" Sophie let out a frustrated groan. She shook her head and looked at Amanda through watery eyes. "I can't make out if the vision is of something that will happen soon, or if it's someone's painful memory of something that already went down. I just know it's scary and it's incomplete." She sighed, her glance falling on the smooth stone at her feet and dreading the unavoidable task of unraveling the rest of the vision.

"Stupid thing!" Amanda muttered, picking up the rock and tossing it into the dying fire in front of them.

"What'd you do that for?" Sophie jumped from her chair and began looking for a stick she could use as tongs. "We need to get it out of there!"

"Why? Wouldn't you rather be rid of it? Not see anymore?" Amanda cried defensively.

"No, Amanda, there's gotta be more! I have to see, because there's a chance this hasn't happened yet! Don't you understand—what if I can stop it?"

"Oh, crap!" Amanda smacked her forehead with the palm of her hand. "If you put it that way…" She hurried to the stack of firewood by the trailer from where she brought two long sticks to fish out the stone. She gave one to Sophie and they got to work.

"This isn't like other times, you know?" Sophie said, focused on giving the stone a clumsy nudge toward the edge of the pit.

"Uh-uh," Amanda said, shaking the smoldering end of the stick in the cool night air before resuming her own poking of the stone.

"It felt like energy was being zapped out of me or something—"

"Do you mean you felt what the boy felt?"

Sophie nodded.

Amanda stopped mid-poke and stared at her. "That's not good, is it?"

Sophie shook her head.

They had poked and prodded the stone so that now it rested well in the outer edge of the pit, cooling.

Amanda frowned, seeming to have arrived at another conclusion. "Did it make you weak?"

"A little," Sophie conceded, and when Amanda's eyes grew wide with concern she quickly added, "Not drained. Mostly, it spooked me because that hasn't happened before."

Scowling, Amanda tapped the side of the stone with her stick.

"I wonder," Sophie said, her eyes flicking toward her friend. "I really don't know much about it, but what if it turns out this is like a poltergeist, or something." She unloaded her suspicion quickly, thinking that the faster she said it, the less important it would sound to Amanda. How she wished her mother were there; she'd done enough paranormal research over the years to place her well beyond the rookie stage Sophie saw herself in now.

Amanda's head whipped around. "Do you mean like a haunting? Or possession?" she shrilled, eyes darting from Sophie's face to their dark surroundings, as if something would jump out at them at any moment.

Sophie shook her head, suddenly wondering if she should've kept her mouth shut. What was she thinking—to lay this on Amanda! "I don't know," she sighed. "I don't know what it is, and I don't know what I should do. What I *do* know is I won't be able to forget this, and if I can't forget it, I may as well do something about it, right?"

"Right. And in—"

A muffled thud made them glance toward the fire. With a sharp intake of breath, Sophie grabbed Amanda's arm, making her jump. The rock wasn't where they'd left it to cool. They stared openmouthed at the smooth stone that had somehow jumped two feet, back into the blaze.

A log broke, and a spray of sparks shot skyward.

"Holy shit!" Amanda cried, shaking off Sophie's hand and rising awkwardly as if to dart away, but Sophie resisted and made Amanda stay put.

They knelt on the ground by the fire, as close as they could without getting singed. "Do you see anything?" Amanda said in a quivering voice.

Sophie couldn't reply. In the center of the burning slag, where the stone had gone back to, the face of a child began to form. He looked like he was four or maybe five years old. His plump cheeks seemed to crack open where tears had washed away the soot covering his whole face. His lost, frightened eyes rested on Sophie as if pleading with her.

"Don't let 'em get me—" he whispered, and Sophie jumped, making Amanda squeal beside her.

"What is it? Do you see something? What, Sofe?"

"Who's gonna get you?" Sophie begged of the child, ignoring Amanda, but he didn't answer. "Please!" Sophie urged, leaning and reaching into the fire as if the apparition could be held, or pulled out of it to safety.

Amanda put her arm across Sophie's chest to restrain her. "Stop it!" she hissed close to her ear when once again, Sophie jerked forward with her hand outstretched. Amanda grabbed Sophie's wrist and yanked it back to keep her from touching the blaze.

"Crap, Sofe! Look at it! It's like the fire has a life of its own, like you're feeding it! It's sucking on you!" Amanda cried.

One second the flames lashed at Sophie, only to recoil in the next, in a bizarre frenzy.

"Don't let 'em get me, Mary," the boy pleaded one last time as he began to vanish. Within seconds, the panic-stricken whimper faded to nothing.

Sophie slumped back and sat on the ground, knees drawn up. "What does this mean?" she said, more to herself than to Amanda. "And who's Mary?"

"What does what mean? Did the fire talk to you?" Amanda said crossly. "You're the witch! If you don't know what's going on, how should I?"

Sophie registered the defensive tone and immediately put herself in Amanda's shoes; she hadn't seen or heard the boy, so unless Sophie brought the re-telling of it down a couple of notches in the creepy scale, Amanda might conclude her witchy side wasn't all *that*, and decide she didn't want to be friends with her anymore. Beside her, Amanda rubbed her own arms, either for something to do or because she actually felt cold.

"It's freezing!" Sophie said, shivering and looking around as if a blanket might appear out of thin air.

"And scary," muttered Amanda. "Let's walk over to the trailer, there's a couple of sweatshirts back there."

Sophie gave the blazing logs a sideways glance. "Let's make it quick, okay?" she said, hoping the boy wouldn't come back while they were gone.

"You know, I had no idea it could be like this," Amanda said, pulling a sweatshirt over her head. "All this time I thought I understood what you could do with your witchy side."

Sophie winced, still worried about the defensive note she'd heard in Amanda's voice and her distressed looks. "If it's any consolation, this is new to me too. It's the first time I've felt anything this strong, and for sure, this is the first time, *ever*, I've had such a clear vision."

"No kidding—what do you suppose moved that rock?"

As they approached their chairs by the fire, another log broke apart and they both jumped.

"Jesus!" Amanda yelped.

"Just a log—it burned through," said Sophie, her hand over her heart, eyes fixed on the flames as she finished straightening the collar of her hoodie.

"Hey! This is my favorite song!" said Amanda, turning up the volume on the portable player by her chair. They had forgotten all about it since Mrs. Hinckley had turned it down during dinner.

"Isn't this a little slow for you?" Sophie smiled, already feeling the music restore a bit of normalcy to the rest of their evening. Together with the crackling sound of the fire, the song glossed over the unnatural noises that had kept them on edge until then.

"Yeah well—it's still *Aerosmith*," Amanda said, rolling her eyes.

They scooted their chairs closer together and sang along to the anthem of devotion; "I don't want to miss a thing," which Sophie liked as much as she loved the movie it had been featured in.

* * * *

Amanda threw one more log in the fire as they unfolded their chairs into full-length lounges. They laid out the two sleeping bags Mrs. Hinckley had left for them and stretched out under the enormous sky.

"The stars are hanging so low," Sophie said dreamily.

"M-mm." Amanda rolled onto her side.

* * * *

Even though she hadn't thought it possible to close her eyes and rest that night, morning came to find Sophie and Amanda asleep. At some point, the fire had died out and the vision had not come back.

"How was it to spend the night under the stars?" Mr. Hinckley asked, stretching his back as he walked toward them.

Sophie gave him a half-hearted, "It was great." While Amanda flat-out declared, "It sucked," as she rubbed her neck. She did not expand on her comments and neither did Sophie.

The rest of the day was pretty much shot; Sophie could think of nothing else but the mystery of the little boy and the gray eyes of his torturer. She went to the back of the trailer and handled every stone Oliver had collected, but not one of them conveyed visual or sound effects. Apparently, it had been just that one, or maybe, she wondered, there had been only one message and since it was delivered, there was nothing else for her to find. "But what's the message?" she muttered. She had only the boy, the eyes of the attacker, and someone named Mary, no locations, and no dates. She didn't know if it was past or future.

Amanda, on the other hand, dealt with her alarm and bewilderment in a completely different manner. She rode her bike like a maniac that day. From the back seat in the buggy, Sophie could hear all the gasping noises and condemnations uttered by Mrs. Hinckley: "That girl's gonna break her neck!" "Slow down!" "Not that way! Oh! Sweet Jesus!" None of it reached Amanda of course, what with the roaring engines of the bikes and buggy, and Amanda being way ahead of them anyway.

While being jostled in her seat, Sophie watched her friend rip through the desert ahead or alongside the sand rail, taking to the air like a witch on a broomstick with her ponytail flying from underneath her helmet, and she felt bad.

Poor Amanda, she thought, overwhelmed with uncanny sympathy for Mrs. Hinckley and feeling more and more to blame for Amanda's reaction, *she's gotta be really freaked out.*

CHAPTER TWELVE

Sophie let out a sigh of relief as she walked through the front door of her house on Friday night.

"We missed you!" her mother greeted her, with a hug.

"I missed you too, Mom… Where's Dad?" she asked, melting into her mother's embrace and crying unexpectedly.

"Oh sweetie… He's on shift at the hospital, remember? What's the matter, my love?"

In her mother's arms Sophie felt like a child again, safe and loved but above all, completely relieved to place her burdens on her mother's shoulders. Mom would know what was happening and she would know how to fix it. Sophie sobbed uncontrollably at first, the tension of the past couple of days finally getting the best of her. She realized she had tried so hard to handle it all on her own, she had built up so much stress she was close to a breakdown.

Her mother soothed her and listened to the broken pieces of the story. Only when she had calmed down did her mother ask her to repeat her experience in more detail as she guided her into the laundry room. Sophie obliged while mechanically dumping the contents of her duffel bag into the washer, not bothering to sort through colors. She poured a cup full of laundry detergent into the machine and closed the lid. Turning back to her mother, who was listening attentively, Sophie recognized the apprehension in her eyes—she also seemed to realize this was unlike anything her daughter had experienced before.

"Well, we'll just have to research the possibilities of a poltergeist and the mechanics of such a phenomenon," Mrs. Becker said decisively while stroking Sophie's matted hair. "But for now, why don't you take a long, hot shower," she added, kissing the tip of her daughter's nose.

Sophie grinned, feeling the weight of dread and anxiety lift a little. "Thanks, Mom," and then, patting her own head, "ugh! I'd forgotten all about it—this is what's commonly known as helmet-head."

CHAPTER THIRTEEN

The hours after her return had gone by with no insights, but as they turned into days Sophie's annoyance increased. She chastised herself for not being able to channel her energy properly to find the answers she sought. She also worried about Amanda, who'd been unusually quiet at school. She seemed so troubled Sophie wished she could take back the whole experience and have her friend back, exactly as she had always been, cheerful and full of spunk.

* * * *

The weekend arrived like a blessing. Sophie needed a respite to just sit at home and think. On Friday night she was ready to relax and watch a movie with her mother.

While clearing the table after dinner, the sound of the evening news came from the small TV in the kitchen. A woman wearing a cream-colored suit held a microphone to her mouth, her hair slapping her face as she strained to make her words audible over the howling wind.

"Can someone get some clean towels up here, please?" called Mr. Becker, trapped in the bathroom with no linens.

"No yelling, please!" Mrs. Becker called back laughingly. "Sophie, would you? I forgot to bring them up earlier," she said, pointing to the pile of folded towels on the counter.

"Sure, Mom."

"*...Investigators are still working on the case that has so many people outraged—*"

"Wait! Sophie, isn't that where you went camping?" Mrs. Becker pointed at the TV, urging Sophie to come look for herself. The location of the news crew was displayed at the bottom of the screen and it read: *Ocotillo Wells.*

Sophie walked back into the kitchen. "Yes, it is!" Sophie stared at the ten-inch screen and her pulse quickened.

The reporter continued, "*...Two weeks ago today, local park rangers began the investigation of the disappearance of five-year-old Justin Stewart from a campground near the Salton Sea—*"

Sophie dropped the towels and clutched her mother's hand as they both stared at the television set, mesmerized.

"...*The boy remains missing. His sister, twelve-year-old Mary Stewart was found at this very spot and she is still in the ICU at St. John's Memorial Hospital. Authorities say Mary remains in a catatonic state—*"

Sophie gasped, "Mary's the little boy's sister, and his name is Justin!"

Anne reached for the volume control and turned it up. "Stephen, honey, will you get down here!" she yelled.

"*Considering the bruises and broken bones left behind by her attackers, it is truly a miracle she endured the encounter with death. Local authorities have nothing to say regarding the motives for the grisly occurrence and much less about the assailants—*"

"What's going on?" Mr. Becker wore his wife's robe and was dripping on the kitchen floor as he looked at the TV over his daughter's shoulder.

Sophie whirled and buried her face on her father's chest. The unexpected revelation of the boy's identity and circumstances had brought back her own experience of it; the sound of his pathetic cries and the infectious fear that had overwhelmed him, and *her*, on the night he went missing.

"*...The parents of the victim have hired a private investigator to assist the local authorities in the investigation of the hauntingly violent attack on their daughter and furthermore, to put an end, as soon as possible, to the torture of not knowing where their son is. If you have any information that may lead to the capture and—*"

It didn't take long for Sophie to decide to call the private investigator. Her parents agreed to be at her side, to lend her credibility, when she met with him. Sophie knew that if she could hold an article of the boy's clothing, see some pictures of him, maybe even visit the young girl, she might see something that would help them discover Justin's whereabouts.

Having seen the eyes of the perpetrator, Sophie knew without a doubt that she would be able to pick off the rest of him, just by touching anything belonging to Justin or Mary.

Chapter Fourteen

Matthew sprang to a sitting position in his bed, his T-shirt clinging to his sweaty body. His heart knocked in his chest as if he'd run a mile and in the dark, his hand groped desperately at something lost to him in ashes. It wasn't even 9:00 p.m.; he'd only dozed for a few minutes! *Pretty soon I won't have to be asleep for the nightmare to begin.*

Matthew pinched his eyes shut and tears spilled; he let out a miserable groan that turned into a sob as he fell back on his pillow.

In his dream, Trent had been taunting him with the body of the little boy. He looked like a stuffed toy in Trent's hand. "Is this what you want?" Trent laughed, dangling the boy by the arm, just out of Matthew's reach. "Well, come get him then."

For the past two weeks Matthew's room had become both his prison and his shelter. Would it ever end?

Trent had been calling insistently and Matthew didn't know how to avoid him anymore.

"Today will you let me go?" Justin's voice invaded him again. The boy's spirit had remained earthbound, just like his grandmother had said of those first ones, when the demon had been young and inexperienced. Abiku had stayed with Trent, he hadn't entered Justin's body—maybe he'd rejected it on purpose. But Matthew knew the boy could not rest until he'd had a proper burial.

On his nightstand, a bulging leather pouch seemed to throb with the word, *Please.* That was the pouch his grandfather had given him years before. Though faintly, it still smelled of the herbs he'd carried in there during their traipsing months in Africa, but it now contained all that was left of Justin.

Matthew knew no peace.

His eyes filled with tears again. The boy's relentless and unforgiving plea haunted him every minute of the day. Matthew's skin scorched under invisible flames that consumed him—he accepted it as atonement, for Justin's death.

"I can't take this anymore!" Matthew hissed. He stood up and shut off the muted television set where the update on the mysterious disappearance of a little boy was airing again.

Matthew sat at his desk and plucked away at his keyboard. Within seconds, the screen populated with the results of his search. "Possession" was the keyword he'd used because he already knew all about Abiku. Now he wanted to be rid of him.

Matthew's eyes devoured the words and in his mind the idea of what needed to be done began to take shape. Sentences, whole paragraphs, jumped out at him, each one a painful stab.

"Bullet through the heart."

"Bleed the body of the medium to drain the chosen vessel of the spirit."

"Destroy the medium only if the spirit is within him."

"Trap the spirit."

"Banish the spirit."

"Kill the medium."

Elbows on the desk, hands on either side of his head, Matthew closed his eyes, feeling weary and out of his depth. *How do I take back all my pussy-ass, passive behavior with Trent?*

The words he'd seen on the screen continued to blink on the inside of his eyelids, like a bizarre marquee announcing an unavoidable special: Kill Trent.

He swiveled on the chair away from the screen and stood up. He paced in his darkened room, and when he heard the phone ring downstairs he yelled, "I'm not here!" before his sister even said it was for him.

Matthew let himself drop into a chair by the window and he cried, looking up at the million eyes that looked back at him from the sky.

They knew what had happened. They knew what he knew.

CHAPTER FIFTEEN

Sophie and her parents went to Phil Benson's office in the neighboring city of Encinitas. He was the private investigator hired by Mr. and Mrs. Stewart to find their little boy, Justin.

"I'm afraid you won't be able to see Mary just yet. I know you were keen to visit with her," Benson said, eyeing Sophie skeptically before shifting his gaze toward her parents. "Hopefully in the next few days…"

Sophie nodded, picturing the poor girl who'd been beaten within an inch of her life. *Catatonic*, the reporter had said, and she leaned closer to her mother who gave her a comforting squeeze.

"So, the next order of business," Benson said briskly, clapping his hands once. "I brought in a sketch artist because you said you had an idea of what the suspect looks like, right?"

"Yes, sir," Sophie said, looking at the man who'd just walked in with a pad and pencil in hand.

"Chase, Sophie. Sophie, Chase," said Benson, and both Sophie and Chase nodded curtly at each other.

"I'm Stephen and this is my wife, Anne; we're Sophie's parents," said Mr. Becker, pumping Chase's hand.

Shortly after, Justin's parents arrived for their prearranged appointment, the Stewarts and Beckers were introduced, brief greetings were exchanged, anxious as they all were.

"Right, let's get started then," Benson hurried them along.

* * * *

Sophie described, as best as she could, the cold gray eyes she had seen and every facial feature she remembered. The sketcher scribbled swiftly as she spoke, and when the portrait was completed, and Chase showed it to her, she shuddered. He was exactly as she had seen him through Justin's eyes.

Sophie knew Benson wasn't pleased with the fact that the only lead he had came from a sixteen-year-old who "saw spirits." Sophie had seen him cringe as she told her story again, for the benefit of the Stewarts, but the fact was he had to take her seriously, for the sake of the case and to keep his promise to Justin's parents that no stone would be left unturned. She tried to ease Benson's anxiety by remaining objective and factual, sparing him the details of the process involved in capturing such visions. As the morning wore on, Sophie sensed that Benson relaxed a little toward her.

Sophie picked up nothing useful from Justin's parents, only flashes of Mr. Stewart helping Justin sit behind Mary on the quad on that fateful night, but as they said goodbye, she let Mrs. Stewart hug her.

"You're our only hope," said Mrs. Stewart close to Sophie's ear. "Please, please help us find him."

Sophie's heart ached for Mr. and Mrs. Stewart. They clung desperately to the idea that Justin had been abducted and was alive somewhere, waiting for his captor to negotiate a ransom. Sophie wanted to believe it too.

While Sophie and her parents met with the Stewarts, Benson's men had gone to work on the sketch of the suspect, but their initial search was fruitless.

"This just means he doesn't have a record," Benson explained. "It would've been great if he was a repeat offender, but it looks like it's a first for him. It'll take us a little longer, but we'll get him."

* * * *

With Sophie's description of the attacker, Benson decided to appoint half a dozen people to go through all the yearbooks in San Diego County, betting the young man they were looking for was a local.

To help as much as she could, Sophie agreed to review yearbooks as well, and within a couple of days, a UPS truck delivered two cartons containing a dozen books for her perusal.

Sophie eagerly set to work and when she completed the fourth book, she went back to Benson's office to return them and to reiterate the fact that they should mostly focus on seniors and juniors.

* * * *

Word of Sophie's involvement had leaked to the press and they spotted her at Phil Benson's office on her way out. Reporters and cameramen accosted her, demanding a statement that would corroborate their information, but neither she nor Benson volunteered any comment on the subject.

Regardless, a somewhat incoherent story was plastered all over the news that night and the broadcast started with the catchy title: *Psychic intervention: Last resort in the desperate search for Justin Stewart.* Sophie turned off the TV.

Chapter Sixteen

June 2000

During Calculus, Trent leaned in behind Matthew and whispered close to his ear, "If I find out any of you've been talking…" He let the unfinished sentence dangle, like a body from a noose.

Matthew cringed. Trent's demands for utter secrecy were becoming more and more threatening. Matthew had already promised to keep quiet—before they even returned to the truck that night he had promised, along with the other three.

With each passing day, Matthew could hide the revulsion he felt less and less. The vivid apparitions and the pleading voice of the boy tortured Matthew without ceasing, driving the guilt of his own silence past endurance. Matthew saw himself slipping into madness and couldn't decide what to do about it.

The irony of his condition was that his sanity hinged on Trent. He must keep Trent happy and feed his confidence in their friendship, at least until he could figure out how he was going to accomplish the banishing of the spirit. It was going to be tough because now there was the girl.

Matthew recognized her on the news report the previous night. She had shielded her face through the whole thing but only at the very end, she turned to face the camera. He saw her for a few seconds before she ducked into a man's arms whom Matthew figured must be her father. But those few seconds had been enough. He knew she was Amanda's friend though he still couldn't remember her name, and the press hadn't got wind of it either.

"We can't just let it be," Trent hissed close to Matthew's ear again.

"What do you suggest we do about it?" Matthew leaned back in his chair, playing the accomplice game.

"I say we find the bitch and fix her," Trent sniggered quietly.

What the fuck! Who is this guy? thought Matthew, shaken up by Trent's words. *Fix her. He means* kill *her.* He leaned forward and rested his chin on his fists, feeling Trent's proximity like a toxic force behind him. Matthew was visited by a sudden desire to knock him off his chair with a two-by-four, right across the jaw. He was sick of Trent.

Chris, Kyle and Nick dealt with the situation by believing in Trent and his reassuring theory that because of the full-face helmets, even if the girl snapped out of her coma she wouldn't be able to pin them down. They didn't know Trent had taken the boy. They thought it was an unfortunate coincidence the boy had disappeared that same night.

Matthew, on the other hand, was gradually reaching the point where he wanted nothing more than to turn himself in—lay out the whole tale to the authorities so that finally, judgment would be passed on him.

"I think we should first find out what she knows…" Matthew suggested, trying to sound concerned and helpful to keep Trent at an even keel. The slightest tilt in the direction of panic and Trent would detonate. Matthew needed to hide his fear for the girl's fate, because as of that moment, her life depended on who found her first.

Matthew heard Trent settle back onto his chair; apparently, he had no further threats to make. He let his thoughts drift to Amanda, the skinny girl he had met a handful of times at the desert and who almost beat the pants off him on her motorcycle. He purposely recalled their most recent encounter at the Pro Shop in Oceanside, hoping to trick his brain into playing back Amanda's introduction to her friend—with the almond-shaped eyes, what's her name? He wanted to kick himself for not having talked to her, it was the same mistake he'd made with Joan.

In a snap, it came to him at last, "This's my girl Sophie," Amanda had said. And from there, Matthew also recalled her saying they went to St. Mary's Catholic School, in Carlsbad.

You have a chance, Sophie, Matthew thought, feeling his heart swell protectively in his chest.

He began to make plans directly, relieved by the mere sense of having a purpose, a clear objective—and how good that made him feel! If he could save her, surely he could atone for failing to save Justin.

CHAPTER SEVENTEEN

"Oh Amanda, I just don't know what I'm going to do… It seems so hopeless!" sighed Sophie, looking at the half dozen yearbooks strewn over her bed. "I can't even remember what the guy looks like anymore…"

"Take a break, why don't you!" Amanda offered readily. "It's gorgeous outside and we haven't been to the beach in forever!" Sophie shot her an arch look, which prompted Amanda to add, "I'm just sick and tired of you all depressed and stewing over this thing, so let's just go to the beach and lay out for a while?"

"That does sound good," Sophie said, lying back on her pillow.

"So, no *buts*, we're going!"

"You know what? Let's!" Sophie gave in, and the gloom magically lifted with the mere prospect of sea and sunshine.

"Okay, so let me borrow one of your bathing suits," Amanda said, going through Sophie's drawers. "Because if I go home to get mine, I know you'll change your mind, right?" She turned to Sophie, casually holding up a bright pink bikini.

Sophie smirked. "Let's hope your brother's not hanging out at the beach today…" knowing perfectly well Amanda wasn't allowed to wear skimpy swimwear.

Amanda's face flushed. "I don't think so… But I got one on him, and I'll tell Mom about it if he tells on me."

Sophie giggled but wasn't tempted to ask what Amanda had on Oliver.

"Do you think your mom will ever let you wear a two-piece suit?"

"Oh," said Amanda, "she already does, it's just that it has to include a ruffly skirt and the top can't be smaller than a sports bra."

Sophie laughed.

The girls walked a couple of blocks to the beach, lugging their beach chairs and a bag with towels and drinks. They settled themselves close to the water and laid out their oversized towels on the hot sand. They placed the chairs side by side facing the water, and sat down to begin the sunscreen ritual.

Sophie placed a spray bottle filled with water between them, for easy access when it became necessary to cool down, and she laid her head back with a sigh, her feet resting on the towel.

"Thanks," she said to Amanda.

"No problem, but, let's not talk about that guy today, okay?" Amanda continued to fuss over the borrowed bikini.

"You got it. It'll do me good to space it all out for a few hours."

"You know, we'll be graduating next year," Amanda said, finally lying back on her chair, though apparently not quite sure the bikini bottom looked good on her in prone position. She adjusted it some more.

"Uh huh—" Through half-closed eyelids, Sophie could see the bikini bottom was straight across Amanda's hips, for the moment.

"So…what are you going to do with yourself?"

"I want to go to college. You know that," Sophie replied, amused by the swimwear dilemma.

"Oh brother! Seriously, don't you want to like, have *fun* before you go do that?"

Sophie laughed, propping herself up and continuing to watch the mad proceedings, "It *will* be fun to get on with my generals."

"I want to take at least one year off before I decide what I—" Amanda stalled and uttered an agitated, "Oh, hi!" as she quickly tied the bikini straps behind her neck again.

Sophie sat up, blinking away the sunscreen that got in her eyes. She wiped her face with a towel and saw a tall, lean boy of about seventeen. He was wearing dark blue board shorts and she could see the golden hair on his muscled legs. He carried a white tank top in his hand and his torso looked brown and well developed.

"Hi!" He smiled.

"Matt, what are you doing out here?" Amanda said—she'd recognized him right away. "Hey Sophie, remember Matt? The one who can't ride his bike worth shit?" Amanda bragged, and Sophie winced although Matthew seemed to take it in stride.

"I wouldn't go that far," he chuckled.

"Nice to see you again," Sophie said, mirroring his smile, her heart all aflutter as she leaned toward him to shake his hand. His eyes were a much darker shade of green than she remembered. She admired them, inwardly reflecting on how much kindness she could see in them.

"Yeah, nice to see you too," he said, holding Sophie's hand longer than required for a simple hello. Jutting his chin toward Amanda, he grinned, "She just got lucky is all—she was on the trail of least resistance."

"Oh please! We're not going to start that argument!" Amanda rolled her eyes.

"Have a seat," Sophie offered, patting the towel stretched before her and trying to ignore the electricity she had felt from the palm of Matthew's hand pressed against hers.

Despite the tingling warmth still lingering, Sophie turned herself off to all other thoughts, especially the out-of-nowhere vision of the gray-eyed man, as she resolved to enjoy the unexpected pleasure of Matthew's presence.

A flash of straight white teeth—a generous smile, as Matthew took the spot at Sophie's feet. Looking thrilled to be there, he said, "Thanks!"

"So, what are you doing out here anyway? Didn't you used to live in Santee or something?"

"What? I can't come to the beach if I feel like it?" he smirked, pausing to look intently at Sophie before adding, "I'm really glad I did."

Sophie looked away demurely and when she next met Matthew's gaze, she fancied his eyes flickered a secret message to her. Sophie's heart beat fast in her chest and she grinned before she could stop herself.

Amanda laughed, "It's a free country, and I guess I'm glad you showed up too."

Feeling suddenly thoughtless—after all, she didn't know what Amanda's feelings were toward this boy—she glanced nervously at her friend, but Amanda gave her a knowing wink that put Sophie at ease. They'll be riding buddies, she reasoned inwardly, until I get better at it.

The hours went by easily and all too soon the sun began to set. When he asked, Sophie gave Matthew her phone number, and he promised to call her. Before they went their separate ways, he gave her a hug that made her shiver head to foot.

Like bad reception on a TV, a pair of gray eyes flashed before Sophie and she sighed, knowing those yearbooks were waiting for her at home and she'd already wasted an entire afternoon. Still, she was starry eyed the whole walk home.

"Was that a good idea or what?" Amanda gloated.

"Oh, I love you!" Sophie answered, planting a big kiss on her friend's cheek. "I hope he calls," she said, squeezing Amanda's arm.

"Duh! He's all but drooling over you. Though I don't know why, since I was the one revealing more flesh, and aren't boys supposed to like that?"

Sophie laughed, feeling like a normal girl again. How alien was that happy sensation, after the four days she'd spent immersed in visions and murder investigations!

CHAPTER EIGHTEEN

Matthew called Sophie the very next morning to ask if she'd like to go see a movie that afternoon. She said yes at once.

After the show, they had ice cream and held hands while they walked on the beach, talking endlessly. As it was Sunday, their day of discovering each other had to end sooner than desired. They reluctantly agreed to wait until the next weekend to see each other again.

"I'll call you every night," Matthew said.

"It'll make time go by faster," Sophie nodded.

He sealed the promise with a kiss—their first one.

When they broke apart, Sophie shuddered. She loved the way Matthew's lips felt on hers, warm, full, sincere. A devilish wink of the gray eyes flashed in her mind, but she dismissed it as a morbid trick of her brain. She bit her lip, feeling responsible for the fact that Justin's killer had yet to be found, likely because she was too distracted to do her share of the work.

"Are you okay?" Matthew inquired.

Sophie sighed and snuggled in his arms. "Yes, I'm fine, but I'm going to miss you until Friday!"

"I'll miss you too."

* * * *

This might be my first real crush, Sophie thought as she turned off the light on her night table. She had only seen him three times but each one had been memorable, in her opinion. She could honestly say she hadn't felt that way before about anyone—never had she enjoyed thinking about, dreaming about, or keeping company with a boy as much as she did with Matthew.

Three days into the week, true to his word, Matthew had called her every night, but after hanging up with him on Wednesday, the romantic haze he'd enveloped her in was penetrated by distressing flashes of what she could only figure had been Justin's fate. The clipped visions of a motorcycle careening almost out of control, and of something like a ragdoll being pitched into a blazing fire, overtook her with the surreal quality of a nightmare. She clucked her tongue, exasperated, and told herself it was her own nerves and her own guilty heart.

Sophie decided the time had come to really get to work and help Benson. She pulled the remaining five yearbooks from under her desk and put them on her bedside table. *I'm gonna get through these before Friday!* she promised inwardly, not wanting the unfinished project to spoil her weekend.

The thought of seeing Matthew on Saturday was enough to dispel the morbid productions of her mind in which, even though Justin had closed his eyes, she could not escape the chilling gray eyes reflecting the flames of a huge pyre.

On Friday night, Sophie and her parents went to a movie, as was their custom, and over ice cream after the show, Sophie told them of the attraction she felt for Matthew. Her parents immediately proposed to have him over for dinner on Sunday. Sophie beamed.

"So, do you and Matthew have any plans for tomorrow?"

"Yes, we do," Sophie offered between spoonfuls of ice cream. "Tomorrow afternoon we're going to Sea World to check out the new dance place they have there."

"That sounds like fun, sweetie."

"Matthew has a thing for underwater creatures. He says Sea World is his most favorite place to go."

"So, between Mickey Mouse and Shamu you'll have year-round entertainment."

Sophie laughed. "Yes, Mom, I already told him how I love Disneyland, so our next big date will be to see Mickey."

"Sounds like you're both going to have to get a job."

"I know, Dad, I'm not expecting him to pay my way every time."

"But do let him open doors for you! And, wouldn't it be better if you guys went to Sea World in the morning? That way you don't waste the whole day."

"We thought about it, but I have a Greek mythology project due Tuesday. I'm working on it with Brock and he's supposed to come by to get a library book I checked out—he needs it for his portion."

* * * *

Sophie put the myth book on her night table and spotted the yearbooks— she still had two more to go through. She checked the clock and glowered; plenty of time to flip through at least one before Matthew came for her.

Sophie's parents had gone to a nursery to buy plants for their backyard. So, she took a quick shower, got dressed and stretched on her bed. She grabbed a book from the stack and began absently flipping the pages; she couldn't focus. She scanned several rows of pictures and caught herself daydreaming about Matthew. Up her eyes traveled to the top of the page again, with a frustrated groan.

When she caught herself going to the top of the same page a fourth time, she closed the book and flat-out gave in to thoughts about Matthew. He'd been so shy at first. But then he had opened to her, and now Sophie considered he was easier to talk to than even Amanda. *Never tell her that!* They had wonderful conversations about their plans for the future, and they had so much fun living out their lives verbally at either end of the phone line. Yet something in Matthew's voice spoke of a lack of hope she didn't understand.

Sophie knew her dreams would come true one day, but when she listened to Matthew, he didn't seem to feel the same excitement or certainty she felt, as if he liked dreaming but was resigned to the fact his plans would never come to fruition. She couldn't imagine why, and it bugged her so much she decided to ask him about it that afternoon, while they were at his favorite place.

She opened the yearbook again and flipped another page. Her eyes landed on a picture of Matthew, like she'd summoned him there with her thoughts! She sat up straight, her pulse quickening as she flipped the book closed to get a look at the cover. It read: *Santee High School.* She turned back to the page her finger was still marking and looked at Matthew's picture with all her attention. A soft smile played on Sophie's lips; what luck to have found this small treasure! His presence, even in a photograph, warmed her inside and out. Sophie put the book at the foot of her bed and lay on her stomach, pen in hand. She felt foolish and silly but couldn't stop herself. She scribbled hearts and stars all around his picture.

She ran her fingers over his face wondering who his friends were, and more importantly, what kind of girls were in his class that she might have to worry about. With this new thought in mind Sophie eyed the pictures of all the girls in the senior class. Except for a very striking blonde at the bottom of the first page, *Joan,* who Sophie was sure couldn't be Matthew's type, she felt no one threatened her prospects. Her eyes passed lovingly over Matthew's face once again, and then the air seemed to go out of the room.

He looked very handsome with his California tan. His light brown hair was long though very well groomed. He certainly had a dashing smile, but it was the kind that didn't touch the eyes.

Sophie frowned at the vacant expression on the handsome face. The eyes were a wintry shade of gray.

CHAPTER NINETEEN

A cold wave of dread washed over her. For a few seconds Sophie couldn't think what to do. *The guy they were looking for is Matthew's classmate? Does he know the guy—are they friends? Dammit! I won't go down that path!*

She closed her eyes deliberately and conjured up the visions. When she was certain she had him clear in her head, she opened her eyes to compare it against what she saw in the book. No doubt in her mind; even from within the harmless page, he seemed to have the power to reach out and devour her.

The legend beneath the photograph read, *Trent Morgan.* His were the eyes she had seen through Justin's.

It also became painfully evident that the flashes of Trent and Justin she had seen during the past week were not an erratic production of her guilty mind, as she had supposed; instead, they were direct leakage from Matthew's thoughts. He *does* know him! A horrible sinking feeling gripped Sophie as she looked again at the silly scribbles she had made only moments before. Angry tears welled in her eyes; she had been used.

Sick about it, Sophie reached in her desk for a black marker. With a shaky hand, she traced a thick circle around Trent's picture and one around Matthew's. She linked them together with a straight line that went across the page over four other pictures.

She made up her mind to go to Phil Benson's office as soon as her parents came back, which should be in the next few minutes. She walked across the hall to the bathroom and closed the door, let the water run for a few seconds before she began washing her face. Someone rang the doorbell downstairs, but she ignored it.

As she splashed water on her face, Sophie wanted to cry but tears would not come. Just this morning she'd been crazy about Matthew and now the thought of him repelled her. *Why would he do this to me? How could he!* She talked herself in circles. She wanted to pull her hair out. *I hope Mom and Dad get back soon*, she thought, suddenly in a hurry to leave the house. The thought of seeing him was more than she could bear, the idea of calling him and hearing his voice made her cringe and yet when she thought of his eyes, she was filled with doubt. Now that she knew the truth, would she see the evil she hadn't seen before?

"But I *have* seen his eyes! Oh, God help me, please!" she whispered to herself.

"Sophie?" Mr. Becker called from downstairs.

"Yes," she replied, feeling automatically relieved.

"Someone's here to see you, sweets."

"I'll be right down," she said, rushing to her room to get the book Brock had come for. She ran downstairs clutching a paperback entitled *Chronology of Greek Myths*.

"Hi Mom, hi Dad!"

"Hey, sweets, what do you think of this ground cover?" Mr. Becker said, showing her a six-pack of blue and white sprays of flowers.

"Really nice, Dad," Sophie smiled.

"Your friend is waiting for you over there," he said, jutting his chin toward the study.

Sophie went into her dad's home office, prepared to dismiss Brock as swiftly as politeness allowed, but no such thing happened. She froze under the archway that separated the office from their living room.

The sandy gray eyes speared her, taking her breath away. She stupidly thought he was even more handsome than in his picture, but she recovered instantly. She was too outraged by the nerve he showed in sitting so comfortably behind her father's desk.

Trent flashed a dashing smile and Sophie's heart jumped to her throat. *He knows I recognized him!* she thought desperately. Her mind raced to the yearbook still open on top of her bed upstairs. No, he doesn't know about his picture upstairs, he just knows I've seen him in visions.

"Not a peep, *sweets*," he whispered, lifting the front of his golf shirt enough to reveal a handgun, tucked in the waist of his jeans.

A rush of heat traveled up Sophie's spine and exploded on her cheeks.

"Your daddy tells me we're working on a project of *mythic* proportions," he remarked with a sinister smile. "I think we'll have to go to the library for a bit."

Sophie grimaced at the unfortunate coincidence and she scrambled to rationalize her options, but there were none.

"Oh, we'll just be a couple of hours," Trent lied to her parents without skipping a beat. "I promise I'll have her back in time for her date, this is purely *schoolwork*, Mr. Becker."

"Oh, nonsense, Brock. School comes first, and Sophie knows that. If there's work to be done, do it right and don't rush it just because there's fun to be had. Right, honey?"

Sophie stood like a stick in the mud. She wanted to scream, but she had a feeling Trent wouldn't hesitate to shoot them where they stood. So, she faked a smile to her dad and then turned to Trent, her eyes filled with venom.

"Thank you, Mr. and Mrs. Becker," Trent smiled, seeming to enjoy every second of Sophie's disgust. "After you," he said—all politeness, motioning for her to go out the door before him.

"Bye, Mom, bye, Dad," Sophie said, waving at them and resisting the urge to warn them. She turned to leave, her heart beating fast in her chest as if constricted, and she wondered if her parents could sense it, if they had any inkling of her dread.

"Bye, Sophie," they called after her and went back to their backyard project.

* * * *

"Are we ready, my dear?" said Mr. Becker.

"Yes, but before I do, I'm going to put the clean clothes away since they've been sitting out for three days and it's almost time for laundry again," Mrs. Becker replied.

"All right, I'll get everything unloaded and when you come out we can lay out this stuff how we want it."

"Deal!"

Anne Becker went upstairs with a basket full of clean clothes. After putting away all her things and her husband's, she went into her daughter's room. She placed two stacks of clean clothes on top of Sophie's dresser and as she turned to leave with the empty basket, she saw the open yearbook on the bed. Noticing the markings Sophie had made, she took a closer look. Mrs. Becker felt her blood drain—her heart pumped on empty and her head spun.

"Oh my God!" she gasped. "Stephen!" she screamed, taking the steps two at a time, clutching the book to her chest as she raced downstairs.

CHAPTER TWENTY

The vibrating pager on his belt flashed the Beckers' number. Phil Benson pulled over to the first phone booth he spotted and made the call.

He hung up with them, dumbfounded by the new development—their suspect had turned up and had kidnapped Sophie. Benson dropped more coins in the slot and dialed his office. He requested Matthew's number and asked to be patched through right away; he hoped to ascertain the boy's degree of involvement. Unfortunately, no one answered, and Benson hung up without leaving a message.

A sense of foreboding descended upon him, but he shook it off as he got in his car, in a hurry to get to Carlsbad and meet with Sophie's parents.

CHAPTER TWENTY-⊕NE

"Where are you taking me?" Sophie asked dryly as soon as they were alone in his truck.

"What? You don't want to know my name first?" Trent mocked her.

Her lip curled, but she said nothing. Her ethics on mind reading completely gone, Sophie brought forth her budding arsenal of psychic abilities, determined to anticipate his plan. She ignored the distracting images of Matthew she picked up, just from being in the truck, which confirmed to her that Matthew had been involved and again she felt sick.

With her palms flat on the seat, Sophie saw flashes of Matthew. She heard raucous, vulgar jabs exchanged between various boys, but of Trent, all she could see were fragments of memories, like a heap of snapshots in a shoebox; Trent scowling at the road ahead, Trent turning the engine off, Trent stretching his back in the twilit desert, Trent glowering at four boys who were throwing items of clothing at each other. One of them was Matthew.

"So sorry your little Matthew couldn't come with us," Trent said, putting a little square piece of paper in his mouth—she saw it out of the corner of her eye because she refused to even look at him.

"I don't think he knows I'm cutting in on him," he said, briskly shaking his head and howling with pleasure. "This stuff sure gets you jump-started!" He offered her a piece, smacking her shoulder with the back of his hand, "C'mon, take it! Believe me, you're gonna need it."

The brief contact sent shivers up her spine and more visions ran amok in her mind; Trent leaning into Matthew during class, whispering to him, Trent watching Matthew from afar as he yanked the chain off his bicycle and climbed on it at a run.

Sophie turned to Trent and glowered at him with unspeakable disgust. She took the paper from him.

"Atta girl!"

Sophie pressed the button that rolled down the window and threw the paper out before Trent could do anything about it. She glared scornfully at him, hoping he'd paid a good amount of money for it.

"You stupid bitch! What'd you do that for?" he said, grabbing her arm.

She freed herself from his grasp—more snapshots, more impressions. Sophie stared at the crowded, northbound 5 freeway stretching in front of them, deliberately ignoring him.

She could find no rhyme or reason to the drug-induced chaos in Trent's mind. But she did detect a rhythm, or something like a pulsating drone Sophie realized acted like a stimulus to him. And behind that pulsating chant, she sensed an embedded message, clearly conveying a purpose to him.

Once she understood what it was, Sophie isolated the chant, which became a hiss, so clear and malignant as to plunge her into a sinister gloom.

Get rid of her, the drumbeat said.

CHAPTER TWENTY-TWO

Better pleased with the new plan to pick Sophie up at her house rather than meet her at the train station in Old Town, San Diego, Matthew borrowed his father's truck and headed to Carlsbad. He had a funny feeling about the afternoon and didn't know if it was nerves or if he was having a premonition.

Justin had been quiet, all morning long; consequently, Matthew wasn't prepared for what happened when he arrived at the Becker house.

Having missed Sophie by forty minutes, he had no way of knowing that Mr. and Mrs. Becker had linked him to Trent, thanks to the book Sophie had marked and left behind.

Mr. Becker bombarded him with questions as soon as he set foot in the house.

Blindsided, Matthew's survival instinct boiled to the surface at once. He was about to defend himself when, like a preternatural kiss, his grandmother blew a thought his way. Then and there, Matthew resolved to take a stand—he would do the right thing this time. A long-awaited relief washed over him at the thought of ridding himself of the tale of the fateful anthropology report and its deadly consequences.

Just as Matthew braced himself for a morbid story-telling session, Benson arrived at the Becker household and the atmosphere changed in a snap. The time had come for serious investigative work. Matthew delayed the moment of retelling his dark tale and focused instead on helping any way he could.

"I have a good idea where he's taking her," Matthew said, shifting uncomfortably under the accusing eyes of the adults in the room.

"Where? For crying out loud!" urged Mrs. Becker, a note of hysteria in her voice.

"San Onofre," Matthew replied. "There is a campground there from where we'd sneak our bikes into Camp Pendleton, so we could ride out to the hills."

"But why take her there? How can you be sure?" Mr. Becker asked coolly, though his body seemed ready to spring if needed.

"Mr. Becker, those hills are very isolated and further inland there's a canyon we liked to go to," Matthew said, a knot forming in his belly at the recollection of other, harmless, riding trips. "He won't be dragging her out to the desert on a weekend, so he'll go to Pendleton where he'll have the privacy he needs. He wants to kill her."

"How do you know that?" Benson asked sharply.

"He told me so," Matthew admitted miserably, struck once again by the certainty that because of his silence someone was about to die. *I needed to act sooner! Trent never sits back, he's in the make-it-happen business, always has been.*

He had grossly misjudged the situation and his power to control it. His eyes filled with tears and suddenly he wanted to die himself.

"What? You knew about this?" said a horrified Mrs. Becker.

"Yes!" Matthew said, angrily wiping the tears with the back of his hand. "He told me about it and I thought the only way I could stop him would be if he believed I was working on her. I told him I would find out exactly what she knew before we took action and he—"

"We? Before *we* took action? Matthew, how can this be?" Mr. Becker now had him by the shoulders. Matthew wished he would knock him unconscious.

"He wanted to find her and kill her last week, sir, he wanted to—" Matthew looked away and Mr. Becker released him.

"We're losing precious time here," Benson interrupted, and they all looked at him as one looks at the voice of reason amid chaos. "The question is, how can we trust you're not in this with Trent, how can we believe you'll take us to her rather than away from her, so he can do what, as you said, he wanted to do a week ago?"

Matthew looked at his interviewers in turn; he could feel their mistrust and he couldn't blame them. Because of him, Sophie was in the hands of a possessed maniac.

"I know you have no reason to believe me," Matthew said in a tortured voice. "But I do love her—"

"Oh, please! And this is how you show your love? You involve her in your morbid little life along with your murdering friends?" Mrs. Becker raged.

"Please!" Benson interceded. "Let's stay focused; the fact is we have no other leads."

Mrs. Becker buried her face in her husband's chest and cried.

"So, what do you suggest?" Mr. Becker turned to Benson with this question.

"I think we need to take the lead we have," Benson replied, giving Matthew a dissecting stare that made him squirm. "Because he has incriminated himself, Matthew is now in custody and it will be in his best interest for us to capture Trent."

"Okay, Benson, then let's do this thing," said Mr. Becker and turning to Matthew he added, "All right, son, we believe you're trying to do the right thing."

Fresh tears streamed down Matthew's cheeks. He nodded at Mr. Becker.

"If we go in through the base in Oceanside, we could get to the canyon before he does," Matthew said, his voice breaking as he spoke.

"That makes sense, if they're taking the freeway all the way to San Onofre, that alone will take them over thirty minutes."

"And then he has to come back to Camp Pendleton on his bike to be able to access the canyon," Matthew said, slowly regaining his composure. "Last time we rode to it, it took us over half an hour to get there from the campground, and we had no passengers."

* * * *

Before they left, Benson put a call to Camp Pendleton and arranged for their party to be allowed in. With the frail trust placed in Matthew, the somber group started their journey. Not twenty minutes later, they arrived on base, where a Jeep was ready and waiting for them along with an off-road bike.

"I'm feeling confident we might be able to beat Trent there. *If* that is where they are headed and *if* Matthew isn't leading us astray," Benson said to Mr. Becker.

Matthew turned his head, feeling he deserved every ounce of suspicion heaped on him.

Benson equipped Matthew with an ear piece. The plan was for Matthew to lead them to Trent. He would ride the bike ahead of the Jeep, keeping radio contact with them. Should Trent spot him first, his suspicions wouldn't be roused by just his friend on a motorcycle.

Matthew welcomed the refuge of the borrowed bike.

Sophie's father and the detective were giving him the benefit of the doubt, and although this was not good enough for Matthew to escape his own guilt, he was glad to be away from them where he didn't have to see the anguish in Mrs. Becker's face. He knew eventually he would have to tell the whole story, and the thought of what that would do to Justin's parents and to Sophie made him want to bury himself alive.

For the time being, everyone believed they were dealing with a violent drug addict, a possibly armed adolescent whose behavior Matthew had tried and failed to curb. What would happen when they learned he'd summoned a demon—yes, such a thing *had* happened! Matthew had doomed Trent, and through him, Justin. And now—better not think of that!

She would be saved. He would save her.

CHAPTER TWENTY-THREE

Trent pulled into San Onofre State Park and parked his truck by the trailer already there. Sophie eyed the large dirt bike and trembled. She'd seen flashes of it already, through Justin, through Mary and Matthew, and the sight of it only did away with what little hope she had this madness wasn't true.

"Don't try anything funny, witch-girl!" he smirked, cuffing her to the truck's steering wheel while he began unloading the motorcycle. She watched him put on some basic gear, a chest protector and gloves. He already had heavy boots on. Then he came back around to the cab, undid the cuffs and dragged Sophie across the driver's seat and out of the truck.

She stumbled behind him, but he yanked her forcefully upward and propped her up against the bed of the truck. He pinned her there with his body. Sophie cringed and turned her face away. Trent reached for his helmet and had to use both hands to put it on. Sophie wriggled out from under him and sprinted toward the freeway, certain someone would stop. But Trent was not about to let that happen.

Sophie didn't get more than ten feet away when he caught her by the arm and flung her around effortlessly. She tripped on her own feet and fell to the sand.

"I told you, bitch! Don't try anything funny!" he hissed, picking her up off the ground and slapping her across the face.

She fought him all the way back to the trailer, choking back the tears. She wouldn't give him the pleasure of breaking down. *God, I hate him!*

Trent cuffed her hands behind her back then lifted her onto the bike. She broke out in a cold sweat. *How am I supposed to hold on once we get going!* She looked frantically around but could see no extra helmets, no extra anything!

Trent swung his leg over, narrowly missing her, and sat in front of her. The bike groaned under his weight and he kick-started it at once. Sophie instinctively pressed herself to his back and her thighs tightened around his backside and a portion of the seat.

"Sweet," she heard him snigger, and Sophie hated him even more.

"Asshole!" she muttered, nauseated to have to touch him. His skin, even through the shirt, sickened her.

They lurched forward on the powerful bike, and Sophie saw no trail ahead, or road to speak of, but Trent tore through the brush as if over flat land. They went under the freeway and headed southeast, to the hills. She clung to him with her thighs, her cheek pressed to the back of his rigid chest protector.

CHAPTER TWENTY-FOUR

As dusk gave way to night, Matthew rode swiftly, looking behind him to make sure the Jeep still followed. The canyon lay a couple of miles ahead.

Just seven months before they'd been there, the five of them, and they'd had so much fun. Matthew could never have guessed then that things would change as they had. Seven months ago, they had howled at the moon, and they laughed and bragged to each other about the stupid stunts they pulled on their bikes. They drank beer and smoked pot, and all of that had been so innocent in contrast with the present.

He felt like weeping over his mistakes and he again wanted to die when he thought of what his mistakes meant for Sophie.

Matthew gassed the bike. "No way I'm failing tonight."

CHAPTER TWENTY-FIVE

Sophie couldn't see the freeway overpass anymore, and although her face was already raw from grating against Trent's back, she felt her discomforts had only just begun.

She thought of how adamant the Hinckleys had been about her wearing a helmet and gloves just to ride their sand rail—they had strapped her to the back seat, making sure she was safe within the cage-like roll-bars. Their treatment of her then made Trent's present disrespect for her life infuriatingly obvious. Here she was on a dirt bike, as a passenger, with no helmet or goggles, or any safety gear for that matter. *I don't even have my own hands to keep me on this damn thing!* she thought, and it occurred to her, *if he's going to kill me, he's not going to take any precautions!* She would have indulged in morbid fantasies about her death, but a torrent of inbound images overtook her.

She realized they were Trent's memories. Without qualms over violating his privacy, she plunged into what she could already tell was the actual staging of Justin's fate. Somewhere deep in her heart, she wondered if she would be united with the young boy on this very night, and a little twinkle of hope lit up her heart; maybe he's trapped somewhere in these mountains, still alive! The thought gave her strength.

Two small hands struggled to grasp the straps of a chest protector, but they were too tight around Trent's waist; instead, the little hands went for the bits of jersey they could grab. They rode fast through the desert.

Trent braked, dragged one boot on the ground until the bike stopped. He got off and flung the boy to the ground like a sack of potatoes, ignoring the pathetic whimpering issuing from him. Trent lit the pre-doused pyre.

Sophie recognized the same elaborate concentric rings where she and Amanda had so recently camped. As the flames leaped to the sky in her mind's eye, Sophie nearly fell off the bike. The familiar drumbeat driving Trent's actions drew her attention to a new piece of information; on that fateful night, the droning rhythm had had no encrypted message, at least not one she could isolate.

A lone conjecture streaked across her mind: His actions are more than drug-induced.

Trent went back to Justin and squatted beside him. He picked him up by the back of his pants and carelessly draped him across his knees. He pulled a small knife from his pocket and admired the sparkling blade. As the dagger made contact with the boy's neck, Trent was knocked sideways.

Justin cried out when he hit the ground. Trent growled. Matthew had lunged headlong at him, but they were both scrambling to their feet now, breathing hard.

"Are you crazy?" Matthew spat out the words.

Trent bristled visibly, like an animal. His eyes reflected the flames but when he spoke, his voice was not his own. "Don't fuck with me."

Matthew snarled and charged. Trent sprang from his crouching position and stopped him in his tracks with a solid kick across the jaw. Matthew fell sprawling to the ground while Trent rushed back to Justin.

He made a swift gash on the boy's neck. Sophie's breath caught in her chest. *The blood began to spill, in spurts at first, but then it slowed. Trent filled a vial with the thick liquid.*

Sophie choked back the tears and she wanted desperately to break away rather than see more of the gruesome act Trent had committed. But reason won out—as fast as Trent was riding on the irregular terrain, she would certainly fall and break her neck if she let go.

CHAPTER TWENTY-SIX

Each time the prospect of losing Sophie crept into Matthew's thoughts, he told himself to stop it. He guided the Jeep into the canyon, hoping he was correct in his assumptions, and berating himself for doubting.

He was banking on what he knew of Trent, and this was the obvious thing for him to do, at least he hoped to God it was.

Upon reaching the top of a slope Matthew spoke into the microphone, "Best use your emergency lights from here on out."

The Jeep's headlights went out and the canyon before him became the dark throat of a beast, ready to swallow him. He blamed himself for not acting sooner, for having indulged in the pleasure of Sophie's company, and for foolishly thinking he could control Trent.

I should've told you everything up front! Please, forgive me—

CHAPTER TWENTY-SEVEN

The bike shook. Sophie instinctively pressed herself against Trent's back and squeezed his haunches with her thighs—she had no other way to brace herself.

She saw: *Justin's panic-stricken eyes. He wasn't dead, but he was very weak after being drained of his blood.*

Trent held the vial at arm's length, admiring its rich glimmer by the light of the fire. He didn't see or hear Matthew get back to his feet.

The deafening, rhythmic pulsation in his brain made it hard for Sophie to concentrate. *Feed. Feed. Feed,* it said. And how different Matt looked through Trent's eyes; beyond the blood pouring out of Matthew's nose and lip, he looked disgusted and afraid, but compassion had flashed in his eyes, and a deep sorrow. Trent saw it too, and Sophie could feel his hatred for Matthew.

In a brief, uplifting moment, her hopes for Justin expanded to include Matthew. Maybe, he hadn't conceived of such a horror.

But he was there, wasn't he?

But he tried to stop Trent.

As much as she would have liked to, Sophie could not follow up on any of those bits of reasoning because the vision would not stop pouring from Trent—there could be no indulging in wishful thinking.

Trent corked the vial and set it on the ground. Keeping his eye on Matthew, he grabbed Justin's limp body, again by the waist of his pants, and without preamble, he flung the boy into the center of the pyre. A sob escaped Sophie's throat, but the roar of the bike's engine drowned it out. *Matthew let out a rage-filled howl. He darted past him toward the pit, but Trent let out a low grumbling laugh that stopped him dead in his tracks—as if clotheslined, Matthew was yanked backward by Trent's iron grip on his collar.*

The sound that came out of Trent, unlike anything she'd ever heard from a human being, startled Sophie out of the vision because it seemed to come from around him as much as from inside of him. She could tell Matthew's reaction had been the same as hers. Feeling the heat of Trent's body through the forced contact between them, Sophie burned with hatred for all the atrocities she had seen him carry out.

"Enjoying the freak show?" Trent muttered knowingly.

This isn't just drugs, she thought again, petrified by his remark. She shook her head and faced the wind to keep her hair from flying in her face.

A jagged canyon loomed ahead; its two long arms seemed to close them in, prompting the horror of her circumstances to hit her anew—there would be no Justin to comfort at the end of this ride.

Only death could be waiting for her in such a desolate place.

CHAPTER TWENTY-EIGHT

Well into the canyon, Matthew stopped at the base of a slope. A couple hundred feet behind him, so did the Jeep. "Kill the emergency lights too," Matthew told Benson, and saw them go out.

"What now?" Benson said.

"We wait."

Matthew walked up the hill and surveyed the dark terrain, hoping for a sign that Trent was approaching, that this was indeed the location he'd chosen. He had been there twice before with Trent and the rest of the squadron. "Commune with the stars, my ass!" he muttered, remembering Trent's excuse then for bringing them here.

"What was that?" Benson said, and Matthew cursed under his breath.

"Just talking to myself," he replied, making a fist around the handle of the hunting knife he'd taken from the station. He steeled himself for what he knew was required of him—it was coming.

Nothing to do but wait now, so to fill the silence in his mind, Matthew indulged in recollections that highlighted what he perceived as his deadly indecision and apathy.

Their past experiences in this canyon had been so harmless compared to what had taken place in the desert that horrific night barely two weeks ago. And he, Matthew, had let it happen. He had let slide the LSD and the cocaine, he had watched from the sidelines as Trent gradually became a maniacal monster, and finally, the servant of Abiku, as he had called himself the night he murdered Justin.

Kyle, Nick and Chris had arrived after the fact, so they believed it was some desert creature Trent had bled and barbecued for special effects. But Matthew had known better. When the five of them sat around the fire, and when Trent divided up the blood into equal portions, he had *known* better! He wanted to throw up while the others drank their gulp. What protective, big brother urge made him keep that information from them? Even now they didn't know.

Matt had brought the shot-glass to his lips, not daring to drink it or even let it touch his mouth, but Trent was watching him, bidding him to do as the rest had done.

At the foot of the slope, though he couldn't make out the Jeep after the emergency lights had been turned off, Matthew knew Sophie's parents and Benson were also waiting for something to happen. Matthew felt the pressure of their doubts rising to him and enveloping him in what was now an all too familiar sensation of remorse.

He looked around the silent canyon. *Where are you, Sophie?* he wondered desperately, as the events of that night continued to play out in his guilt-ridden mind.

There was no telling how much LSD Trent had taken that night, he was hallucinating bad. Chris snapped out of his drunken stupor to say, "What the fuck's wrong with him?" But Trent ignored him or simply didn't hear anything as he continued his summons to the fire and smoke, as if participating in an eerie two-way transmission. Matthew stared at the shot-glass in his hand—it was still full, it still felt warm. The flames leaped, the smoke funneled skyward. Arms outstretched, Trent called out: "Abiku!"

Matthew froze.

"Drink it," Trent ordered.

CHAPTER TWENTY-NINE

It was useless to try to stop the visions. Sophie kept her eyes shut tight as she jostled against Trent's back.

"Abiku commands it—so drink it, fucker!"

Matthew's surprise at the mention of the weird name was evident. He made no verbal refusal; instead he flung the vial containing the last share of Justin's blood into the center of the fire. He looked defiantly at Trent, and Trent growled in return.

His arms reached for the sky again, and he called on Abiku once more. The flames leaped as if commanded by Trent's voice.

Sophie's head was spinning; she couldn't make sense of Trent's words, but it seemed he was surrendering into the hands of Abiku. She knew not what it meant, but that character had been popping up in his mind throughout the night.

The smoke rising from the fire took on a very distinct shape—the shape of a man with smoldering eyes and a crooked mouth. Trent bowed down to it, oblivious to his friends' looks which suggested he might have lost his mind. But the creature thrived on Trent's reverence, and it responded to him with a welcoming gesture of its smoky arms.

The other boys couldn't see what Trent saw, that was evident, but Sophie wondered as to the validity of this vision. *What if I'm seeing his hallucination rather than what really happened? Is that even possible?* She could do nothing but wonder.

Unexpectedly, Trent leaned forward into a jump, leaving Sophie unsupported. She lost her balance and flew off the bike. She hit the coarse ground with a gasp. Her hip ached, and her arms became badly scraped as she tumbled over clumps of prickly sagebrush.

Trent stopped a few feet ahead and slid around to get her. He undid the cuffs and ripped her off the dirt as effortlessly as she had seen him do with Justin. He made her get back on the bike, ignoring her complaints. He too climbed on and cuffed her wrist to his own.

Although unhappy about the direct contact with his bare skin, she appreciated the more secure feel of this arrangement. Trent took off abruptly, forcing her to grip his waist with her free arm.

The vision resumed, and Sophie focused almost immediately on the apparition Trent had summoned out of the fire.

The disturbing shape of the man had no stomach, or more explicitly, there seemed to be a hollow where its stomach should have been. The significance of this escaped Sophie, but her notice of it was more unnerving than any other vision so far.

High in the evening sky, the moon spread its silver beams over the serene desert. The squadron sat by the fire, enthralled by the flames—likely coming down from their high. Matthew, eyes glazed, his face frozen in an expression of terror.

Justin had been consumed by the blaze and all that remained were his small bones. As for his precious innocent blood, there was not a trace of it left. The rite had taken place and Trent seemed to have experienced a release after having pacified Abiku's hunger.

Joined at the wrist, her pain mingling with sweat, dust and blood, spurred the clarity of the vision and Sophie knew, she felt it; Trent's conscience bore no guilt or sense of wrongdoing. He felt he had done his duty and was infected by a sense of accomplishment that seemed to warm his cold heart.

Trent raked through the smoldering remains and picked out Justin's bones from the pit; they were the smaller ones from his hands and feet. He divided them evenly between the four, like a priest, smugly handing out consecrated wafers, pleased to see the reverence with which they were taken from his hands, until he gave Matthew his share, and suddenly it was not so.

The flames leapt to the sky once more and Trent's serene, clear-headed state vanished. He convulsed, reacting to an invisible force that struck and shoved him backward. A stream of objections and apologies issued from him, "I did as you told me," *he cried in desperation that quickly changed into fear.* "I did what you asked, the way you asked! No, no it shouldn't matter—I couldn't stop him—Yes, but the rest of us did take—Why should it matter that he didn't? I did as you said!" *Trent's pleading with the invisible something went on and Matthew, as if dreading what might come next, backed away, but continued to watch Trent from a distance. The other three sniggered at Trent's meltdown.*

Was it pity she had seen in Matthew's eyes? Yes. And an acute understanding of the kind of ritual that had taken place, which he'd been too late to prevent.

The walls of the canyon hemmed them in; the constricting darkness heightened her imagined difficulty breathing. Trent slowed down, and Sophie was silently thankful; the cuff cut painfully into her wrist and the ache from her bruised hip seemed to spread all the way to her neck.

Over and over, the hopelessness of her predicament assaulted her; she was tethered to Trent and there was nothing she could do—even if she managed to free herself from the cuff, Trent could overpower her, he could outrun her, and he would most certainly outlive her on this night.

CHAPTER THIRTY

Matthew glanced toward the bottom of the slope—it looked deserted. He strained to see the Jeep, knowing it had to be there, and in it were Benson and Sophie's parents, waiting, just as he was.

Silence settled over everything like a dense fog. Matthew filled his lungs with a deep breath. He exhaled and gazed at the witnessing sky; the stars transported him again to that night.

He picked up the bones meant for him, which Trent had spilled on the ground. Trent continued to rave incoherently after the initial convulsion had sent him sprawling backward. Matthew feared but also hoped Trent would end up jumping into the flames at any second. He held the bones in his fist and stood up, unable to decide which feeling was stronger within him; that of his guilt, or the revulsion he felt for Trent. His lunch came to the top of his throat, and it burned sourly in there.

As swiftly as it started, Trent stopped convulsing and pleading. That was enough to put Matthew further on edge. The flames subsided, and the silence was a blessing but only for a few seconds. Trent's eyes bugged out as he scanned the horizon. The beams of light were distant, and the sound of sirens reached Matthew in a muffled wave. Completely composed now, Trent ordered the retreat, but not without first casting a condemning look on Matthew.

Matthew was first to catch sight of a headlight and he heaved a sigh of relief. He had been right, and Benson and the Beckers knew that now. "Let's hope he stops close by," grumbled Benson in Matthew's ear.

The racket of the bike was all he could hear as he followed the erratic beam of light. If only he could get some indication of Sophie's condition!

The bike stopped where Matthew had figured, and an eerie quiet settled over the scene. Then, "Get back here, you bitch!"

"She jumped!" Matthew hissed but didn't wait for a reply from the Jeep. He could see Trent about fifty yards below, spinning his bike furiously, shining the headlight in different directions.

"I'm going after her," he said, figuring that by now, they would have split up to find Sophie as they had agreed to do if she attempted to escape.

She'll be okay, Matthew told himself, willing his words to have the power to make it so.

He continued further down the slope, in the opposite direction from where Sophie's parents had gone. Benson, the only armed individual of the party, would be headed straight for Trent.

"C'mon Sophie, be alive!" Matthew whispered.

Fortunately, Trent was so loud in his conviction that he was alone that Matthew was able to advance without worrying about stumbling and panting in the dark. He scanned the random path of the headlight because, other than falling over Sophie, that was his only chance to spot her. Matthew was about twenty yards from Trent when he slowed his pace to begin combing the ground for her.

Light swept over the tufts of sagebrush, revealing nothing but dry earth and rocks. Matthew could sense Trent's anger and frustration, so he kept a level head. He called her name in strenuous whispers, hoping she would hear him. Out of the corner of his eye he saw something shift under the passing beam, only thirty feet from where he stood. But Trent had seen it too and he turned to shine the headlight on the same spot.

Matthew froze; he couldn't beat Trent on foot.

The headlight bounced over the rugged terrain toward Sophie. Matthew watched the advance, his heart beating in his throat.

CHAPTER THIRTY-ONE

As soon as Trent stopped the bike and announced they'd arrived, he undid the handcuffs. Quick as lightning Sophie swung her hand, with the cuff still dangling from her wrist, and struck his temple. Trent doubled over, covering the side of his head with his hands and letting out an angry howl. She took advantage of the few seconds her stunt afforded her. Thanking God for her quick reflexes, she vanished in the dark.

The headlight swept toward her; she dove to the ground and froze for the fraction of a second it took to pass over her. She began crawling with renewed energy, ignoring the thorn on the palm of her hand, fully aware that he might have seen her. Her fears were confirmed, and in an instant, he was coming after her. *He'll expect me to move away from him*, she thought, and despite the rough, clay-like dirt, she at once began lizard-crawling diagonally, toward him. *Move faster—gotta move faster!*

Having avoided his direct path by about twenty feet, she crawled furiously in the direction Trent had started from. Even with the flood of adrenaline, Sophie could not escape her discomforts; her chest felt too small for her beating heart. Her rib cage felt exposed, as if the skin had peeled away from dragging herself in the dirt. Trent passed not five feet from her; the ground beneath her rumbled, the blaring engine rattled her insides, and for a few blinding moments she was enveloped in exhaust fumes and dust.

Sophie rolled over on her back to catch her breath. The night sky, with its dim orange tint on the horizon, taunted her with the knowledge that city lights shone there, like a blanket of safety that wouldn't reach her.

"Sophie, answer me if you can hear me!"

She heard the urgent whisper and wondered how it could be Matt? She held her breath.

"Sophie, he's gonna come back this—holy shit!" Matthew stammered as he stepped on her and fell back in surprise.

"Ugh!" she grunted, curling onto her side. "What are you doing here? Have you been here all along?" she whispered.

Matthew crouched down beside her. "No, Sophie, please! I'm trying to help you. I went to your house to—I told your parents— They're around here somewhere, looking for you too," he explained.

"Yes, but how?"

"C'mon this way," he urged.

They crawled side by side, trying to steer away from Trent and his bike.

"You fucking bitch! I'm gonna find you and when I do, I'll make you sorry!"

"There's a Jeep and a motorcycle over that way," Matthew said, leading the way.

Sophie followed. "I think he's backtracking now," she said, knowing there could be no contest but somehow hoping, after all, her parents had come for her—Matthew had brought them!

The headlight found them.

Matthew stood and helped Sophie up, edging protectively in front of her as they turned to face Trent.

"You're both dead!" he spat.

Sophie looked over Matthew's shoulder. "He has a gun," she warned him.

Trent pulled the handgun from his waist and aimed it at Matthew. He fired a shot from about fifteen feet and it sent them both flying sideways to avoid it. Sophie screamed, and Trent circled back to them to take a second shot.

"Halfway up the slope," Matthew groaned, "there's a bike—you have to get to it!" The bullet had grazed his right shoulder.

"But Matt, I can't!"

"Run!"

"I can't leave you!"

"Now!"

Sophie took off just as Trent's light shone in their direction again. She heard another shot, but she dared not stop. Her heart seemed to fracture with the certainty that Trent had killed Matthew. And he would now be coming after her.

Where the hell is that bike! she cursed inwardly, stumbling and groping in the darkness. She could only see about ten feet in front of her, her thighs burned from the uphill strain and her pants rubbed the bruise on her hip, sending raw chills all through her.

Trent's headlight swept in her direction once again and she panicked. She turned to see how close he was, and breathed a little easier when she saw he was still too far back. She changed direction and kept running, but she was stopped short with the dull pain of her body crashing into something hard. It knocked the wind out of her and she fell on her backside. Gasping for air, she suddenly she realized that the object she had struck was a bike.

She managed to get on her feet, taking air in miniscule amounts as her diaphragm permitted, until the spasm finally wore out. Meanwhile, Trent drew closer.

Sophie's apprehension toward the bike was soon conquered by her fear of death. "Here goes nothing," she muttered, swinging her leg over the bike as she had seen Amanda do, except Amanda was taller. Fortunately, the bike was leaning against a boulder, which made the whole transaction a little easier.

He would spot her in the space of a heartbeat.

"This thing better start first try!" She kick-started it and the bike bucked and stalled. "He left it in gear—jerk!" She instantly regretted cursing Matthew, believing him to be dead. She did her best to channel Amanda's stories and operational details before she tried it again.

This time, the bike started, and Sophie revved the engine. She didn't turn on the headlight because she figured she was better off not seeing where she was going, and Trent would not be able to see her as easily.

Trent's headlight found her anyway. He charged.

Sophie put the bike in gear and took off. She discovered at once the relevance of keeping her rear end off of the seat when in rough terrain. She hoped none of her teeth were broken after the first landing jolt that took her by surprise.

Trent gained on her easily and she was certain she heard a bullet whiz by her head.

"That asshole is shooting at me!" she raged, and yet she stupidly recalled Amanda's description of the exhilaration she felt when she rode her bike. Sophie finally understood it and what was more, she agreed.

She swerved left and then right. Sophie didn't know where she was going, all she knew was that she *had* to keep going. Her thighs were shaking and so were her calves from holding herself up. Her arms were killing her, and the realization that her life depended on how long her limbs could sustain her was of no comfort to her.

She circled back in the direction she came from, hoping she would run into her parents and between the three of them maybe they could knock Trent down. But the bike went over a mound of dirt big enough to send bike and rider flying. When she landed, she lost her balance and her right foot couldn't find the foot peg. She wiped out and the bike fell on her leg, dragging her a few feet and causing painful scrapes on her back. She managed to free herself, but Trent was now towering above her as she writhed in the dust.

Her face was badly scraped and bleeding from various abrasions. Her right leg throbbed but she didn't think it was broken.

He dismounted and limped toward her. As he walked into the light she saw him take aim. Her eyes fastened on his bleeding outer thigh. That's why he's limping! A surge of hope warmed her. She remembered Matthew said her parents were around.

"You pissed me off!" Trent hissed; his voice had a strange, twitchy quality.

"You killed that little boy!" she screamed.

"In life there is a purpose for everyone. Happy are those who fulfill theirs!" he scoffed, cocking the gun.

"You deluded psychopath! You killed Matthew too and even if you kill me tonight, you will pay for what you've done," Sophie said, scratching at the dirt, trying to loosen the clumps.

"Just shut up and die with some dignity! I've had it with you!" he snarled.

Sophie flung a fistful of dirt at Trent's face.

He howled in exasperation and fired a shot that made Sophie shut her eyes, waiting to find out what it felt like to have her brains blown out, but she felt nothing.

He'd missed! She opened her eyes, perplexed by her good luck. She stood up and scrambled over to where he was, stamping the ground and wiping his eyes. She grabbed him by the shoulders and brought her knee up to his groin as hard as she could. But Trent didn't double over like she hoped he would; instead he backhanded her across the face, sprawling her backward and causing a spray of shiny dots to temporarily blind her.

She shook her head and got back on her feet, feeling a little disoriented.

Trent was on the ground, on all fours, heaving. Apparently, her kick had a delayed reaction. He raised his eyes to her, appearing fierce even in his current state. She approached him with caution.

In the same instant he started to raise the gun, she delivered a kick that caught him square in the chin, at last rendering him unconscious.

Sophie heaved a sigh and she noticed Benson for the first time, his gun poised and ready to shoot if Trent should try to move. Benson kicked the gun out of Trent's reach and prepared to cuff him. That's when it happened.

Trent rolled onto his back. His eyes snapped open and a rumbling snarl, as of many angry wolves, erupted from him. He sprang up squaring his shoulders, ready to lunge at Benson, who staggered backward in shock.

Sophie too backed away. Surprised by the arms which materialized from the darkness, attempting to hold her, Sophie let out a frightened yelp and twisted on the spot to see who had her.

"Sshh, sweets, it's us," said her father. But Trent's attention turned toward them, as if drawn by their voices.

His smoldering eyes fixed on Sophie. Dust swirled in the beam of the fallen bike's headlight.

"You'll not destroy my high priest," said the rumbling voice. "I am Abiku," it declared. The evil eyes rested on each of them in turn.

With animal-like agility, Trent charged Benson, the only one of them who was armed, going directly for his neck.

The two men wrestled to the ground. Grunts and growls issued from them like two rabid dogs bent on killing each other.

The attack had been so swift Sophie and her parents were just beginning to react, when another gunshot silenced it all.

Trent lay motionless on top of a panting Benson. Matthew stood six feet from them, with Trent's gun still aimed at the body. Everyone seemed to hold their breath, then a thundering roar rent the air.

Trent's inert body quivered, imbued with supernatural life. It rose several inches into the air, twisting and jerking to a standing position, three feet above the dirt.

Shocked, Benson scrambled on all fours away from him. Sophie didn't have to look around to know the others were all gawking too.

Trent's mouth opened at an unnatural angle as he let out a tortured howl. His neck snapped with a nasty crunching sound and a viscous black mass erupted out of him. It pulsated over Trent's head to the rhythm of the shrill cries of the unspeakable voices within it, united in wrathful protest at the death of their priest.

Sophie put her hands to her ears and shook her head, her eyes shut tight.

Chapter Thirty-Two

Matthew blinked away the vision of the cotton-headed high priest who looked on the scene, shaking his head and clucking his tongue pitifully.

Then, the voices and the black mass holding Trent erect twisted in a wringing motion. Trent's head and torso convulsed until, with a final harrowing bellow, the mass was sucked out of him as if by a vacuum. It corkscrewed east like a taut spring being released. The echo of the voices reverberated in the still air for the space of a heartbeat, and then there was nothing.

Matthew lowered the gun. Trent's empty body dropped to the ground with a dismal thud. The blazing stare dimmed and at last disappeared, leaving only Trent's vacant gray eyes, reflecting the beam of his bike's headlight.

CHAPTER THIRTY-THREE

Matthew took the pouch containing Justin's bones out of his pocket. He offered it to Benson, stammering, "Would you, please—make sure…"

Benson held out his hand to receive it. He seemed to weigh the contents of the pouch for a moment while giving Matthew an appraising look. "I'll see that this is returned to Justin's parents," he said, putting it in his coat pocket. "We'll sort this out, son," he added, putting his hand on Matthew's shoulder.

Matthew's eyes clouded with tears. "Justin will be able to rest now."

Benson gave his shoulder a fatherly squeeze. "Thank you for stepping in."

Matthew sat in the back seat of the Jeep with his head in his hands. Sophie climbed in and took the spot in the middle, next to him. Mrs. Becker sat on the other side, behind her husband.

Sophie reached for his hand just as Benson started the car to take them back home.

"You tried to stop him," she whispered, "I saw it."

A painful lump formed in Matthew's throat. He couldn't bear the tone of absolution he heard in her voice; he should never be forgiven for what happened to Justin!

To see Sophie safe, to have her alive and next to him was more than he felt he deserved.

The Jeep jostled on the dirt road and Matthew gave Sophie's hand a squeeze, wanting to convey, in that one gesture, all that he regretted. He couldn't speak; he could only let the tears run down his face.

When Sophie's warm hand squeezed his in return, Matthew felt his heart would explode with both guilt and relief. He looked up and caught Benson's eye in the rearview mirror, and the detective's eyes smiled approvingly.

Matthew leaned his head against the window and his shoulders shook in silence.

He felt Sophie scoot closer; she put her head on his shoulder, and her hand over his chest had a soothing effect. "Thank you for saving my life," she said, her voice breaking a little as she spoke.

"I love you," Matthew whispered hoarsely, "So much."

THE END

A CURSE LIFTED

Patricia Bossano

Experience the power of a parting gift—one I will be grateful for, for the rest of my life.

The objective was simple enough—I had to get through the black tunnel, reach the door, and open it.

Brilliant light bulged from gaps around the door, making it look like a fiery arch and confirming the fortune-teller's promise: "The answers are on the other side." If only I could get there and bust the door open.

I moved forward.

The walls of the black tunnel seemed to throb all around me, letting me know I'd soon reach my goal; only a few more steps and I'd get to the light.

Then, a blunt certainty struck me—there were no black walls around me!

The tunnel was a sentient thing, an inky blob thudding to the rhythm of my imaginary footfalls, deceiving me; feeding the illusion that I was moving, when in fact, I was standing still, in the dark.

My heart beat faster and my nerves prickled with the realization. Something inside me said, "Gotcha," in a wheezy growl that put an alien fear in me.

"Stop," said the fortune-teller, causing the pulsating blackness to recede.

I opened my eyes and squinted at the bright candles she had set on the small table between us. She sat sphinxlike, her Egyptian features gleaming ominously. Her black eyes glinted in the candlelight, her dark hair spilled from beneath a do-rag strung with brass coins.

Disoriented, I glanced around. The tangerine light of the autumn sun as it set burst through the splintered blinds of the street-facing window, making the cramped space seem ablaze. The rumble of traffic on the Pacific Coast Highway gradually reached me, dispelling the carefully crafted psychic mood within the shop.

For the last ten minutes, I'd been inside my head and had forgotten that I was in a twenty-dollar-a-reading palmistry shack in Dana Point. After months of passing by it, I had finally given in to temptation. As for the palm reader in front of me—well, I had paid her not twenty, but forty-five dollars to make good on her claim to show me the portal into my past lives because, "Just by looking at you," she had bragged, "I can see three of your previous lives."

She had rattled off enticing tidbits about a medieval whirlwind romance, torn to pieces by greedy relations who wouldn't part with *my* riches. She told me about the quiet Greek existence I had once led, devoted to temple rituals. She also said I spent a lifetime as a missionary, in a jungle; I had exiled myself there to mend my broken heart.

With such a preamble, how could I resist handing her the money?

"What did you see?" she asked, leaning forward and letting the candles make odd, upward shadows on her face. I got an eerie sense that she already knew the answer, like she'd been right there with me in the tunnel.

I told her what I saw and, though it made me shiver to remember it, I also told her what I thought I heard: "Gotcha!"

She sat back, nodding wisely, which increased my discomfort.

At length, cocking her head to one side, she announced, "When your mother was pregnant with you, a curse was placed on her. Do you know who may have had a grudge against her?"

I said nothing for several seconds as I digested this. But the fortune-teller's cold, dry fingers on my hand made me jump, and I burst into speech.

"No! I can't think of anyone who'd want to hurt my mother." But even as I said it, I thought of my beautiful mother, and how much jealousy beauty like hers could engender. That she still lives in a country where witch doctors and spiritualists are revered, and spells and curses are everyday occurrences, made me even more doubtful.

She nodded again, like she'd been listening to my words along with my thoughts.

"Patricia," she said, with an earnest tone she hadn't used before. "It was the dim aura around you that alerted me."

I listened warily, feeling self-conscious about the news of my aura being dim. Where was she going with this?

"I could tell you were blocked," she announced.

I must have looked affronted because she launched into an apologetic explanation. "I see you as one who should shine like the sun, but something is stopping you, and I wanted to find out what it was."

As casually as I could, I extricated my hand from under her fingers.

"I have never seen such potential," she added, leaning over the candles again. "You are meant to see through, backward, forward, and beyond!" she declared.

I leaned away from her.

"It *is* a sentient thing," she said, as if rummaging through the images in my head, and plucking that particular one, in her effort to convince me.

She's good, I thought, even as I shook my head.

"That's the curse, that's the block," she assured me.

"I don't know if I believe that," I stammered, but already I was inwardly agreeing with her; I *did* have potential, I *should* shine like the sun.

And all the inklings I'd had, throughout my life, of such power, now seemed to morph into proof that I'd been wronged!

There must have been a curse.

To her detriment, she drastically changed tack and got down to business, causing my conviction to waver and ultimately fizzle out. You see, for the bargain price of five hundred and seventy dollars, which would be spent, for the most part, on blessed pillars and cleansing oils, she would teach me to fight the curse, so I could eventually be rid of it.

Feeling let down, but also relieved, and having nothing left to say, I stood up and shook the fortune-teller's hand. I promised her I would think about it and took the proffered business card.

She had me going, I thought resentfully, because for a few minutes I had entertained the possibility that I wasn't insecure, that I didn't have confidence issues keeping me from great achievements—I was cursed, for crying out loud!

But, how effective can the removal of a karmic roadblock really be, if performed for financial gain? And for all I knew, she might have uncovered the curse only to fill her income quota for the month!

I rejoined my friends, who'd been waiting for me in the tiny area adjacent to the chamber where I was nearly swindled out of my hard-earned money. I jutted my chin toward the door, giving them an arch look. As we crossed the Pacific Coast Highway, out of earshot and on our way to our dinner reservation half a block away, I told them the details of the visit. The whole time, my eyes kept darting back to the neon *Palmistry* sign—I swear it was winking at me.

As we leisurely approached the restaurant, the upper arch of the moon cleared the Capistrano Beach hilltops, and by the time we ducked in for dinner, the full moon was out, bathing everything with its milky glitter.

I let out a sigh and laughed under my breath, *Curse, my ass!* and congratulated myself on having resisted the urge to spend nearly six hundred bucks on candles.

Although... Could a curse be blinding me, on purpose, to the possibility of being rid of it?

Nah...

* * * *

One year later, I sat at my desk at work, looking distractedly out of the window, where a mamma bird had made a nest. For the past three days she'd been diligently pecking at my window. Again, I told myself I should bring bread crumbs to sprinkle outside, within her reach.

It was Friday, and I felt inexplicably anxious—could it be because, for the first time in my adult life, my parents and my godmother, Cristina, were coming to visit me? I would be hosting them at my house, like a grownup!

Yes, that was probably it.

My mom and dad had flown in from South America to make a round of visits to all the relatives here. They had been in Colorado with Cristina for a few days, and as of this morning, they were on their way to San Juan Capistrano.

The mamma bird tap-tapped at my window, and my mind drifted toward musing comparisons.

* * * *

On my dad's side, relationships with the extended family never seemed to overstep anything, and early on in our lives we grew accustomed to the caste-like degrees of separation. In stark contrast, my mom's side of the family is boisterous, tight, numerous! My mom has three brothers and six sisters, and everyone knows everybody's business.

Also, there is definitely a sketchy trait, a radar of sorts, between the ladies that allows them to know, or see, things happening to others in the bosom of the network, from one hemisphere to the other. We've dubbed that superpower, *el correo de las brujas*—the witches' post.

That closeness has been in their blood—our blood—since infancy, and it matured through their childhood on a farm in Ecuador. By the time they began migrating to the United States, they had the network down.

Soon after they met and married in New York, my parents opened their doors to my mom's brothers and several of her sisters, to help them make a start. Their humble beginnings in a crowded apartment, the hard work, the laughter, disappointments and victories, only strengthened their bond.

When my two sisters and I came into the picture, it was into the arms of, not just my mother and father, but the whole clan coexisting in the household—Cristina, Jenny, Bria, Gavin, and Albert.

As loving as our whole family is, we are not without our quirks. For instance, my generation is resignedly aware that the matriarchs will always see us as their little hatchlings, no matter if we're married (which I am) or have children of our own (which I don't, yet). If they come into our homes, it is to indulge us in a session of playing house where we try to act self-possessed but are doomed to fail under their scrutiny of our domestic skills.

But, back to my anxiety over whether or not my kitchen was clean enough—I did change the sheets on the beds. *Shoot!* I know my mom will hate the cat—I'll vacuum one more time before they show up! Must calm down—there really is no reason to stress about it.

It was two o'clock in the afternoon when the phone startled me out of my bird-watching and reflections.

"This is Patricia," I said, while the mamma bird pecked at my window again.

For a few seconds, nothing came from the other end of the line, but then I heard my mother's voice. "*Mija*," she sobbed.

Mind reeling, I glared at the bird. Each of her pecks said, *death*. I knew this! I had always known a bird pecking at your window signals death. I'd learned it along with my bedtime prayers—just like what to do with spilled salt.

"*Mami! ¿Qué pasó?*" I cried. What's happened?

"We crashed," she said, and on hearing the words, my heart felt so constricted I thought I might die. "I haven't told anyone yet, but your Aunt Cristina… I believe she's dead."

Tears sprang from my eyes. How can it be? It cannot be!

The bird blinked at me, then she flew off.

* * * *

For the next few hours, my mother's desperation, her fear, her sadness shrouded me in a haze of depression as I made flight arrangements to get to Denver that very night.

I arrived at my aunt Cristina's house to find my two sisters, several cousins, aunts and uncles already there. We had mobilized as one.

My father, who'd been driving the car, my mother, and Cristina's body, were expected to arrive from Grand Junction the next morning. I would see *her* in the afternoon.

* * * *

In a haze of disbelief, we arrived at the funeral home for the viewing. There was Cristina; she wore a peach-colored dress, beautiful against her perpetually tanned skin. She had bruises and cuts on her arms and hands which the makeup had failed to cover completely. I knelt beside her, not knowing what to do about the oppressing sensations crushing my chest or the bitter feelings ravaging my spirit. I reached for her hand and held it even though the thick, unresponsive feel of it sent a thrill of fear through me—I placed a tremulous kiss on it anyway.

I cried in silence, not knowing what prayer to say, so I talked to her instead. I told her how much I loved her. She was my godmother! Cristina was the coolest aunt I had, and she was gone, leaving a gaping hole in the family's bosom.

I loosened my grip on her hand then grabbed it again. The warmth of mine, which had transferred to her skin, tricked me into believing—if only for a second—that it had all been a horrible mistake, that the life-giving blood flowed through her, warming her once again. But it was not so. Over and over, I thought, *I love you*, convinced that her soul would sense what her ears would never hear.

Unthinkable though it was, the moment came when we had to leave Cristina there for the night.

In a fog of bitter realization, we gathered at her house; family, friends, neighbors, and together we embarked on hours of remembrance marked with tears of despair and, at times, laughter, as we all shared treasured recollections of Cristina's boundless energy and her ability to inject humor into any situation.

Near midnight, after those who were staying elsewhere left and we tidied up the social areas, it was time to say goodnight. Tomorrow we would bury her.

My older sister, Raquel, and I headed for the basement (our assigned sleeping quarters in the crowded house). We brushed our teeth in the small bathroom, exchanging silent, tearful glances in the mirror. When we finished, I hugged her, and we said goodnight. I turned off the fluorescent light as I went to my side of the room.

I got into the sofa-bed and sighed, remembering the couple of seconds at the mortuary during which I believed Cristina had come back to life. I hated and loved those seconds. The sting of tears came at once.

The loud click of a switch preceded the room brightening with the glow of the bathroom light. I waited to hear Raquel moving around in there, but all was quiet.

A little disconcerted, I climbed out of bed and went to investigate. I peeked in the bathroom; empty.

I flipped the light switch off again and returned to bed like a sleepwalker, with my arms stretched in front of me, as all I could see were bubbles of light in the darkness.

"Hail Mary, full of grace," I began, but had to pause as the bathroom light turned on again. My hand went to my mouth and I waited in the silence, suspecting I wouldn't hear my sister.

Once more, I got up and turned off the light. My heart fluttered in my chest as I got back into bed. Almost immediately, the light turned on again. *It's Cristina*, I thought, my eyes darting wildly over the stark white walls, looking for I don't know what.

My breath came in short spurts, but still, the corners of my mouth quivered upward. It *is* Cristina! I told myself.

Scooting to one side of the sofa-bed, I lifted the blankets and patted the empty space beside me, inviting her. *Please come*, I prayed.

Nothing happened.

I so wanted to hear the creaking of the bed, which would signal she was joining me. I held my breath for even a whisper from her. Nothing.

I propped myself up on the pillows, determined to wait her out. It didn't take long.

A prickling sensation began in the small of my back, and I shuddered. I sank deeper into the pillows, but kept my eyes open wide. I wanted to see, feel and hear anything and everything that was about to happen.

My eyes were suddenly drawn to something moving above me. My breath caught as I looked up. There on the white ceiling throbbed an inky black mass, big as a night table. I turned hot and cold, and then hot again. I didn't know what to make of it.

As I stared, the thing coming from somewhere behind me continued to slither across the ceiling. Thunderstruck, I watched its slow pulsating progress toward the small window across from me until it squeezed through it, and slid out of sight, into the night.

I sat there, wrestling with my thoughts—what the hell was that about? I hadn't a clue! I shook my head at the idea I may have imagined it. "Not possible—I saw what I saw!"

The bathroom light shut itself off, making me jump, not just because of the loud clack of the switch but because of the impenetrable darkness it left me in. It was like someone saying, "Show's over. Go home, people, nothing left to see."

Or go to sleep, I thought. And against all odds, I slept.

* * * *

My cousin Johanna, Cristina's oldest daughter, gave a beautiful speech during the funeral mass. Her voice didn't falter once. I remember thinking how very brave she was, how strong in the middle of such a tragedy. How very beautiful, even though the light seemed to have gone out of her eyes.

When the singing resumed after Johanna spoke, I saw my father stand up from his seat beside my mother—the service wasn't over. He gave her hand a squeeze and walked outside.

María, my younger sister, elbowed me. I took the hint and followed him at once.

The sight of my father, alone on that bench in the empty churchyard, broke my heart. His shoulders shook uncontrollably, and I raced to his side. I held him while he sobbed like a child.

"It should've been me!" he said at length, wiping his eyes with the back of his hand and taking deep breaths. He felt responsible! The moment's guilt seemed to weigh physically on him, like a presence.

"*Papi*, no! It was an accident," I argued, understanding that he might be feeling unequal to facing those of us who had survived Cristina, as if we'd rather it had been him. "No, *Papi*," I repeated. "That is not true."

Only minutes before the car hydroplaned in the wild rainstorm that surprised them, Cristina had left the middle seat of the van, telling my mom and dad she was ready for a nap. She had curled up on the back seat, and snuggled with a pillow, "To dream about my *flaco*," she'd told them. *El flaco* being her tall, skinny husband.

My dad patted the side of my face and through fading sobs he murmured, "I've said what I *needed* to say—I've said what I needed to say."

* * * *

We laid Cristina to rest.

Once again, tears and laughter marked our third night of grieving. Every single one of us had a story to tell about how she touched our lives with her irresistible vitality and wit. But as the witching hour drew near, the house grew quiet.

Standing around the kitchen counter with my two sisters and my mother, we listened to the rest of the family's footsteps, upstairs, settling into their beds.

The experience of the night before came back to me then, and I repeated what had happened with the bathroom light, and what I had seen.

"Patricia!" Raquel exclaimed (of the three of us, she's the one with the best memory), while my mother looked thoughtful and María's eyes went from one of us to the other. "That is exactly what you saw when the fortune-teller tried to walk you through that tunnel, remember?"

I gasped, "Holy cow!"

María nodded too, but my mother looked blank. I had told Raquel and María the story of what happened in Dana Point the year before, but I hadn't said anything to my mom. So, I repeated the details of my failed attempt to access my past lives and finished with, "What I saw last night looked exactly like the black stuff surrounding me in that tunnel!"

The three of us looked expectantly at our mother until she nodded slowly. "It was your Aunt Cristina who turned the lights on," and then with more conviction, she added, "She wanted you to see. She wanted you to know the thing you thought was blocking you had *left*. Cristina got rid of it for you."

Tears welled in my eyes. This was true—it couldn't be otherwise. Whether that sentient blackness had been a curse or a morbid projection of my poor self-esteem, my godmother, having reached that place where all answers shine bright, gifted me with a powerful visual riddance of it.

* * * *

I kissed my mom and María goodnight and headed to the basement, a strange serenity pulsing inside me. Raquel and I brushed our teeth and hugged each other before we went to our beds. I pulled the covers under my chin and began to say my prayers. The bathroom light stayed resolutely off.

"Amen," I said, and for a moment I saw myself lying in bed, in the dark basement, gradually beginning to glow until I was completely blanketed by a golden radiance, nowhere near dim.

I smiled. I didn't need to open my eyes to know my aura was restored to full brilliance.

* * * *

Several months later, I happened across the Egyptian fortune-teller, her impressive mystic demeanor significantly watered down by being in such mundane a place as the local mall. I caught her eye, brow raised, but did not approach. She nodded with a knowing smirk.

The understanding passed between us—I was whole.

* * * *

As for the in-utero curse itself and who cast it, Mami said she couldn't think of anyone that could or would have done such a thing. But Raquel and I exchanged wary glances; we both had a name in mind.

That's another story though.

205 ½ 25ᵀᴴ STREET

Patricia Bossano

Staircase to *The Rose Rooms* at, 205 25th Street, Ogden, UT

After a forty-minute delay the plane at last takes off from San Diego.

I'm on my way to Salt Lake City and feeling a bit shaky, not because I'm flying—I've made this trip countless times for business—but because today, when I finish my meeting with a customer, I'm driving to Ogden, or Junction City as it was known back in the railroad days.

Kendra, a local realtor I called a week ago, had readily agreed to show me the vacant property at 205 25th Street. A realtor's willingness to humor a possible buyer shouldn't be taken as a sign of anything other than said agent looking for her next commission, but I wanted a sign that I was doing the right thing by digging into the past, so I took her enthusiasm as the universe saying, "You're on the right track."

Despite all that, I'm still unsettled by the upcoming prospect of at last walking through the place where a woman I never met used to live.

The first time I heard her name, Rosetta Duccini Davie, I was four or five years old. My grandmother had introduced her by stating that my mom and I owed our lives to Ms. Davie.

I didn't know it then, but this was a many-layered story my grandmother would deliver, piece by piece over the years, according to her strict definition of age-appropriateness.

During my elementary school years, she told me Rosetta had been a beautiful woman, "raven-haired and red-lipped," Grandmother said, "and the kindest soul in the roughest of towns," which Ogden *had* been in the 1940s—too rough even for Al Capone, some say.

My grandmother had dozens of stories about Rosetta, which she repeated to me whenever I asked.

Often, Rose was my bedtime story, and I began cementing her in my mind and heart as the ideal woman for me.

I had no trouble seeing Rose exactly as Grandmother had: a wealthy lady, driving her fancy black Lincoln, or walking her pet ocelot up and down 25th Street—or Two-Bit Street as it used to be called. Rose had been noticed and admired by everyone in Ogden, but most of all, by this elementary school boy—decades later—who nursed a secret crush for the rich woman who helped those less fortunate, and who couldn't stand the sight of animals being mistreated.

Grandmother told me Rose and her husband, Bill, were well known for their business ventures and their passionate romance. I had mixed feelings about Bill—I tried to fit him in as a father-figure in my childish fantasies, but I gave it up as I got older and mostly ignored that she'd had a husband.

Most of my grandmother's descriptions of Rose leaned toward the portrayal of a saint, but there were offhanded bits about her that stood out, drenched in color, in my ten-year-old mind. To me, Rose was a glamorous goddess, the lion-tamer in the rough circus-like world I imagined she lived in.

It wasn't until I got to junior high that I got a more detailed explanation as to *why* my mother and I owed our lives to Rosetta.

Grandmother told me that in the 1940s she had worked at a doctor's office in Ogden, to help her struggling family. Her dearest hope then had been to marry her charismatic beau of one year, whom she loved with all her heart. Convinced he would eventually propose—after all, he wasn't in the Navy anymore and was a self-made man—my grandmother allowed their intimacy to progress, until she got pregnant. When he found out, "He simply disappeared," Grandmother said with a distant look in her eye, and I had a feeling that, maybe, he had come back at a later date. But she didn't give me a chance to even ask, she just went on to say, "I was only twenty-two and I knew perfectly well that my family would put me on the street if I turned up pregnant—which they did."

Dejected and ashamed, my grandmother decided she wanted to abort the baby, but Rosetta, who knew her from the doctor's office, convinced her not to go through with it. "You see, Rose couldn't have children of her own, and she was not about to let someone she knew commit such a crime."

The day my grandmother made that confession is burned in my mind. "I couldn't have lived with myself if I'd gone through with the abortion," she said, and I remember thinking I'd never seen such remorse and sadness in someone's face. The decision she made, even if she ended up *not* doing it, weighed heavy on her, and I think it tormented her until the day she died.

After my mom was born, Rose made sure Grandmother had extra cash, food and clothing to help raise the baby. "If it hadn't been for Rose…" Grandmother would start but could never complete the sentence. I think her circumstances had been so dire then, she simply refused to dwell on them in the present. She would just shake her head and cluck her tongue, "Rose was an angel!"

"And what about the father, my grandpa, did he ever…?"

"Never you mind about him," she'd wave me off the subject. "He died a long time ago, never even met his daughter. I heard, though, he died in 1982, same year you were born, and they threw his ashes in the ocean."

It took me a minute, but I understood what she was saying—she'd kept track of the man, and I realized she must've really loved him. I

151

would've asked about it too, if not for the typical warning look that said: "No more questions about that!" And that was fine by me; whatever curiosity I may have had about him paled in comparison to my fascination with Rose, even though all I had of her was a black-and-white image, cut out from a newspaper, which my grandmother had preserved in plastic since the '50s. "The spitting image of Rita Hayworth," Grandmother would say, and I would nod, star-struck.

It wasn't until my mid-twenties that I found out who Rose really had been, and all I can say is that the knowledge was as disconcerting as it was satisfying, on one count in particular; I finally learned why my mother never shared the same fervor for Rose that my grandmother professed.

Rosetta Duccini Davie and her husband, Bill, had owned and operated the classiest establishment of ill-repute on Two-Bit Street, known as The Rose Rooms—at 205 ½ 25th Street.

Dozens of questions queued up in my mind when Grandmother made the revelation, but the dynamic between us only allowed for her to say what she wanted while I held my tongue. She did share, among other things, that Rosetta had been a stickler about all her girls having monthly physicals at the clinic where my grandmother worked, which at least rectified my original misconception that Rose had been a patient there and that was how they'd met.

It took me three years to come to terms with the fact that the woman I thought of as a saintly goddess had been a madam all along, and only now have I worked up the courage to see the place where Rose, my ideal woman, lived and did business all those years ago.

Sometimes I wonder if Grandmother lived at The Rose Rooms for a time, after her family refused to take on another mouth to feed. I think my mom wonders the same thing, but Grandmother died, possibly thinking I'd never be old enough to know that… And I still wonder about my grandfather—she never told me his name. Did she really never see him again?

* * * *

My meeting went well, though I think I was distracted. All I could think of was getting in my rental car and heading north—my head was full of Rose.

* * * *

I exit the freeway on Thirty-first Street and proceed north, on Wall Avenue, to the Union Station. I turn left onto 25th Street, and on the corner of Lincoln and 25th, I see the brick exterior of The Rose Rooms—the windows on the second floor seem to gape at me.

There is a parking spot right in front of number 205, and as I pull into it, I'm thinking that the ½ used in the address back in the 1940s must've referred to the second floor, but they've dropped it now.

I stare giddily at the glass door on the left side of the building and I can't help thinking, *I'm here, and through that door and up the stairs, The Rose Rooms wait for me.*

Anxious for some fresh air, I get out of the car and I breathe in and out, hard, like I'm warming up for a run, as if suspecting that what's coming might rip my breath away. I'm itching to be inside, but Kendra isn't here yet, so I press my nose to the cloudy glass and see a steep though wide wooden staircase with two landings, brick walls on both sides of it. At the height of the second landing, there's a door to the right.

I won't pretend the altitude is responsible for my heart beating faster. I know I'm spooked.

Rosetta and Bill lived up there, is what I'm thinking when I get taken over by a weird sense of time flashing backward and forward, so fast that it may as well be standing still. In a matter of seconds, I catch an eyeful of everything that was—like a flash of memory, quickly erased by a vision of what could be.

A tap on my shoulder startles me.

"Sorry," says the woman who'd made me jump.

"Hi—yes, sorry," I stammer, trying to focus on her face, but all I see is the hint of that door on the second landing. I force myself to say, "You must be Kendra."

She beams. "Yes! It's good to meet you, Fernando."

We shake hands and make small talk. I tell her I didn't have any trouble finding the place and she apologizes for the unseasonable heat. "After all, it is April in Ogden, and temperatures should be cooler," Kendra says. I nod at this, but I don't tell her that I'm here precisely on the thirtieth anniversary of the death of a family friend.

It's a far-fetched coincidence anyway, I tell myself, though the idea that Rosetta died on April 21, 1980, in Tampico, Mexico, where I know the weather is hot that time of year, keeps taunting me.

"I have a client a few doors that way," Kendra says, pointing up 25th Street. "She has some questions about a lease agreement we worked on, and I thought I'd clear things up with her, since I'm here."

I'm already nodding. "No problem."

"I'll let you in and I'll be back in twenty minutes tops," she assures me cheerfully, digging through her purse for the keys to The Rose Rooms. When she finds them, I take them from her and open the door.

As I return the keys, Kendra says, "Look around all you want, you can't hurt anything in there. Just don't trip over stuff—it's kind of messy."

"No worries, and thank you," I reply as she hurries up the street, and I turn back to the wooden staircase.

The door creaks closed behind me as I step in and begin to climb.

Out of nowhere, the thought hits me about the hundreds of men, all those regular johns, who must've come up these steps with paper money in their pocket, looking for a little companionship, and I have to ask myself: Am I jealous—begrudging them their pleasure?

"I'm not going to the work rooms where tricks were sold," I mutter, "I'm here to see Rose."

At the height of the first landing, I detect a flowery scent, something like jasmine, which comes as a surprise inside this old building in need of renovation.

By the time I reach the second landing, I can't shake the feeling I'm completely unprepared for this.

Frustrated, I cross the threshold, taking in every bit of the dusty, ransacked surroundings. I walk toward the center of the room and accidentally step with half my foot on a two-by-four on the floor. I counterbalance and before I know it, I'm flat on the ground, the back of my head is throbbing.

It takes me a moment, but I stand up and slap the dust off my pants, glad Kendra wasn't there to see me do what she said not to. I look around and realize reason must have left me completely, because I'm now in a lavish chamber decorated like a Chinese restaurant.

There are black lacquered surfaces everywhere, silver foil wallpaper with pink flowers covers one of the walls, and a mural has been painted on another.

A spotted cat slinks beneath the two windows opposite me and leaps onto the top of a piano, side-stepping a picture frame and a vase with flowers, which have been placed on the black instrument.

Cold sweat breaks out of every one of my pores.

I look away from the cat, processing the fact that it might not be a cat at all. Hell! Inside the Rose Rooms, it would have to be an ocelot!

The alarming suspicion that I have walked into another dimension overwhelms me, but I can't turn back. For a moment, I'm paralyzed—only my eyes swivel, taking in the sight of Rose's living space.

Near the center of the room I see a table covered in a red cloth. There are six chairs around it. One of them has been pulled out and I know I am invited to sit. I do so and exhale, relieved from the burden of standing.

I sit there in the silence, hands on my knees, trying to stop the shakes. My eyes are glued to the sleepily blinking ocelot, wondering if a brain scan is in order as soon as I get out of here.

The slightest creaking sound issues from the chair next to me, the air vibrates and, as I hold my breath, it begins to take shape—and it is the shape of a woman.

I've never passed out in my life, but I think this is it for me. I recognize her! I know that long dark hair and those fiery eyes. Her creamy skin glows, and her red lips look like a wound on her smooth face. Rose.

I know I'm out of my mind, at once believing and disbelieving. I can't look at her without a jumble of thoughts racing through my throbbing head—

I owe Rose my life.

She's the most generous soul that ever lived.

She's a madam and a lion-tamer.

She's an angel.

And she's sitting right next to me.

Her experienced fingers knead my thigh and then begin working their way up. This is torture.

Again, I picture the men who paid for her touch, and I hate them. Instinctively, I press my legs together, feeling this is my only defense against her insistent progress. Part of me wonders why I should bother defending myself, but the rational—Catholic—part of me yells, "Run!"

"*Mierda*," I mutter (this means "shit" in Spanish) and her laughter rings in the room, or maybe just inside my head.

"I have missed you so, Billy," she purrs, and I'm foolishly glad she's not laughing at me. Her husband Bill, being half Mexican, like Grandmother said, must have used the expression on occasion, and I had just reminded her of him.

A sense of guilt rattles me at that moment, and right away I feel like a teen making out with his girlfriend while the parents are away. Terror grips me; what if Bill shows up and finds us? But she called *me* "Bill."

Do I look like him?

"He died the same year you were born," my grandmother whispers from her grave.

I'm not *her* man. I'm not Bill—jealousy and disappointment feel like a punch to the gut.

A growl, something straight out of *The Exorcist*, comes from the corner of the room where the ocelot sits on top of the piano. I freeze.

"Don't mind her, it's just Gata." Rose nuzzles my neck and I feel her tongue there—tasting me. "She's in heat..." she says, her mouth opening over my ear. She lets out a heated moan full of longing, making me shake from head to foot.

Shocked by how quickly my state of arousal is escalating, I stand up abruptly, knocking the chair backwards. "Mierda!"

My rash reaction has hurt her feelings, I know it as soon as Rose looks up at me, her eyes wet with tears and a pout on her lips that makes me want to carry her off to a bed, and eat her up with kisses. But I can't do that, because if do, it will mean I have lost myself.

"Billy," she sighs, her voice full of pain and my heart aches for her, *and* for me. Bitter jealousy pokes at me—I'm not her man. But didn't I used to be her husband?

I hesitate. Her eyes plead, and I can't swallow the knot at the top of my throat. My eyes water and she becomes blurry at the edges. Rose looks down at her hands on her lap, and I see silver tears splash on them.

"Oh, Billy," she says.

Unbearable. I scramble to my feet and back out of the room, avoiding the two-by-four this time.

Splaying my arms toward the brick walls for support, I stumble down the wooden stairs. I feel dizzy, possibly because I can still feel the heat of her breath. I can hear the longing in her voice. I can see the fire in her eyes.

Out on the sidewalk, Kendra is not back yet. I look back at the stairs through the glass door—what would happen if I went back? What if I tried to touch her? Would she say *my* name if I asked her to?

For a few rapt moments, I think I will! I might just buy the building, live in it and never see the light of day again.

"Go back and do it," says a voice inside my head, "she is the woman for you, isn't she?"

I walk a few steps back and forth; I know I'm talking myself into acting like a madman. And I want to! I've been alone too long, and I need a woman with me. I need Rose.

The distorted reflection on the cloudy glass stops me short. I recognize me, but I also see the man that had just *escaped* from The Rose Rooms—am I remembering right? Did I have to scramble to my feet?

I did! The jarring recollection makes me pause. Stricken, I consider the fact that I had been lying on the floor, *because of the damned two-by-four!*

My brain screams this couldn't have been an unconscious experience. I can still feel her. Even out here, there's still jasmine in the air—and that lustful stirring! But my shoulders sag as I exhale.

In the warm orange radiance of the twilit sky, the spell, the hex, the curse, whatever the hell it was, begins to loosen its grip on me.

Refusing to look back at 205 ½, I lurch across the street to a bar called Kokomo. I take a seat by a murky window and ask for a shot of tequila.

As soon as the surly waitress brings it, I gulp it down. Grimacing, I signal to her to get me another; if this doesn't quiet the riot in my mind, I don't know what will.

Through bent, grimy slats I squint at the brick face of The Rose Rooms; the front windows gape at me slantwise, resentful—like I got away or something, and I can't help feeling, I probably did.

The third shot of tequila dulls my senses nicely, and oddly, my thoughts become clearer.

Across the street, Kendra just went up the stairs and when she doesn't find me up there, she'll come back out, so I leave a few dollars on the table and head back to wait for her.

* * * *

"Oh! There you are," Kendra smiles, closing the door behind her. "So, what did you think about the building?"

Instead of shaking my head, I nod agreeably, mechanically, and words I hadn't meant to say come out of my mouth.

"I think the space is perfect for a bar." Stricken again, I wonder what happened to the sober epiphany of a few minutes ago; that I would find my own raven-haired, red-lipped Rose, among the living! Obviously, it left me completely in the time it took to cross 25th Street.

"Oh! That's a great idea! There used to be a tavern on the first floor of the building, you know. And above it, there was a brothel," Kendra offers smartly as she hands me a book. "I picked this up for you when we set up the appointment; it was published just last year, and it has the whole scoop on this building and more!"

The front cover reads *Notorious Two-Bit Street*, and from beneath the title, Rose smiles seductively at me.

Seeming to notice what caught my eye, Kendra taps the image and chatters on, "That's the madam of The Rose Rooms, and they say her husband, Bill, was really keen to own the tavern downstairs too."

Perplexed by the existence of this fresh evidence, I open the book to a random page and my glance falls on, "Bill died…in 1982…cremated by the Neptune Society…ashes buried at sea…had been in the navy prior to his marriage to Rose."[2]

I snap it shut. "I don't want anything removed, even if you think it's debris—I want to go through all of it myself before renovations begin."

---

[2] *Notorious Two-Bit Street* by Lyle J. Barnes, p. 196-197

When you next visit Ogden, be sure to stroll down notorious Two-Bit Street, that is, the stretch between Washington Boulevard and Wall Avenue. When you get to the corner of Lincoln and 25th you'll see the brick façade of The Rose Rooms, now the bar and nightclub, Alleged.

Take note of the bathroom doors and the base of the main bar on the second floor; you'll see all the original doors from the "trick rooms" were put to good use.

Salud!

* * * *

Factual tidbit about *205 ½ 25th Street*

The legendary raven-haired, red-lipped Rosetta Duccini Davie was the seductive madam of the most elegant brothel on Two-Bit Street in the mid-1940s, known as The Rose Rooms.

Despite her chosen lifestyle, Rose was known as a kind-hearted, generous individual. She loved animals, as evidenced by her many pets, including an ocelot named Gata, she loved to cook, and she was passionate about helping people in difficult spots.

When tasked to research a story for the *Tales from Beyond* anthology, the excerpt below was what inspired me to write *205 ½ 25th Street*.

"At one time, she learned about her doctor's nurse, a young pregnant woman who intended to end her pregnancy. Rose went to see her and talked her out of aborting the child…baby clothing, food and other provisions began appearing at the front door of the young mother's apartment…[she] suspected Rose of placing the provisions there…"[3]

For more fascinating insights into Rose's life and her infamous rise and fall, I highly recommend reading [3]*Notorious Two-Bit Street*, by Lyle J. Barnes.

CAROLINA BLUE

Patricia Bossano

An anguished scream, a wisp of blue…She's on the railroad tracks

Friday, November 13, 2015
Despite it being Friday the thirteenth, my daughter and I threw caution to the wind and decided to go shopping at the Gateway in Salt Lake City. Crossing the tracks to wait for the Front Runner train I heard a distant scream. I turned south, toward the old Union Station, and saw a wisp of blue.

* * * *

November 21, 1924

"Amelia, be a dear and take care of this," her boss said, handing her a lumpy canvas bag.

She took it and began pulling out several women's garments while her boss continued to talk.

"Mary's out sick at the hotel so they got no one for this fancy washing," he said, eyes swiveling from her to the laundry she was piling neatly on top of the presser.

"Yessir," Amelia murmured, taking out the last item and letting the empty bag fall to the floor. Oblivious to her boss watching, she fingered the chiffon dress, dazzled by the lovely Carolina-blue fabric.

"Belongs to a lady stayin' at the hotel—guess she's on her way to San Francisco day after tomorrow or som'n. Wants her stuff cleaned 'fore she goes."

For sure a movie star, Amelia thought, unable to take her eyes off the delicate thing she now held at arm's length. She admired its scoop neck, the wide ribbon gathering the chemise at the waist, and the heavy skirt with— she counted them, seven slits. It was the most beautiful thing she'd ever seen. "Yes, sir," she said again.

Amelia's boss nodded and left her to it. From there, fate seemed to take over.

She felt thankful for the cool November air coming through the windows—it was hot as H-E-double L among the pressers and steam generators inside the laundry building. All Amelia ever washed and pressed were the linens from the sleeper and diner cars stopping in town, so this was an unexpected treat. She was quite conscientious with the dress and spent over two hours on it, not minding the task one bit.

As the day drew to a close Amelia's eyes darted with increasing frequency toward the dress hanging on the coat rack in the hall, across from all the machinery. She'd covered it with a white sheet to protect it.

The blue dress is just under there, she kept thinking, and she wondered too if her boss would be delivering it to the hotel that night—surely, he would.

Something unpleasant stirred within her at the thought, and it made her frown.

The steam generators had been turned off, the washers too. It was very quiet in the laundry building. Amelia usually left with everybody else, but not tonight.

She paused in front of the rack, took her time putting on her coat and stared at the white sheet while she buttoned herself up. She imagined the blue chiffon beneath. Amelia bit her lip as she put on her hat and was ready to leave, but she couldn't resist. Inching closer to it, she ran her fingers down the length of the sheet. It's just under here…

In the silence, thinking of nothing but what a fine thing it would be to wear such a dress, Amelia lifted the sheet, took the dress and hastily wrapped it in paper—the kind they used to pack up pressed napkins. She nestled the bundle in her work bag and turned to leave.

When the night watchman spoke, her heart fluttered. She hadn't heard him come in.

"Not feeling so good, Sam," she said shakily. "Might not be in tomorrow." Amelia walked past him, clutching her work bag to her chest.

"You get to feelin' better, wouldya?" he called after her.

"I will, Sam, good night."

Amelia walked briskly, holding tight to her "borrowed" treasure. The two blocks to her shabby dwelling on Lincoln and 25th seemed like nothing in her feverish state. All she wanted was to wear the dress once. She barely acknowledged her landlord's greeting grunt, hurried past him and ran up the rickety steps to her rented, dingy room.

Just the one time, Amelia said to herself, *and* to the dress, as she hung it on the window latch.

The dress seemed to reply with a pleasing vision Amelia eagerly dived into: *In the daylight, her shapely calves and knees were visible as the breeze twirled and flapped the panels of the Carolina-blue skirt. Her feet were encased in a pair of T-bar shoes.*

Amelia looked under her bed. There sat the very pair of shoes—the only pair of nice shoes she owned, which had belonged to her mother. The smile drooped from her face as reality hit her afresh; had it been two years already?

Losing both parents and her sister, all in the same day, sure had changed her and the world around her.

Shaking off the recollections, Amelia picked up the shoes and polished them, so they'd shine. Tomorrow would be her *one* day.

Somehow, despite her anticipation, Amelia slept.

The sky was growing light when she opened her eyes, and the first thing she saw was the Carolina-blue chiffon. Jumping out of bed, she went to wash herself in the common bathroom on her floor. Back in her room, she pulled the dress from the hanger and slipped it over her head. It didn't surprise her that the dress fit as if it had been made for her. Glad for the unseasonably warm November day, because she didn't have a nice coat to wear over it, she sighed and felt reassured she'd done the right thing.

Amelia looked at herself in the cloudy mirror one last time and beamed, "All ready."

She opted for the back stairs of her building so as to leave unnoticed, certain that no one would recognize her once outside. So, off she went to the dedication of the new depot at Ogden's Union Station.

Dressed like a fine lady, Amelia meant to enjoy the day as such. She even had an extra dollar to eat out and maybe get herself an ice cream cone.

She made her way to Union Station where the town's best had turned up for the ceremony in which thirteen Ogden Society Girls would drag the train, by ribbons, into the station. Locomotive Number Two stood at the north end of the depot, with the colorful ribbons already tied to it. After a quick glance though, Amelia counted only twelve ladies present.

One of the photographers turned from his camera and spotted Amelia. Her surprised smile broadened, and as if summoned by it, he came to where she stood behind the ropes. He held out his hand and Amelia took it. She let him lead her to the cluster of vivacious ladies waiting to perform the ceremonial pulling of the train—a delicious warmth lingered on her skin after he released her hand. The girls eyed her up and down but seemed to accept her as one of them, likely taking her for an out-of-towner, which suited Amelia just fine.

After the photograph was taken, he could not be persuaded to leave Amelia's side. They strolled arm-in-arm to the Union Station Restaurant where they lunched together. "I intend to make the most of the short hours we have," he said, and Amelia's spirits soared.

He even bought her an ice cream cone before he left on a train to the East Coast, and from there he would sail back to Italy.

That night in her bed, Amelia giggled. They had talked about nothing for hours, yet that had been enough for her to feel she knew Stefano inside and out. She had given him the post office's address and he promised to write often.

* * * *

Over the next twelve months, Amelia received a letter every other week from him and she wrote back faithfully. The day she received the clipping from his newspaper in Milan, *La Domenica del Corriere*, she laughed out loud, amazed by the colorful, full-page illustration from the photograph Stefano had taken. Not only that, he had fixed to it a scrap of paper with a translation of the Italian headline:

"Curious American Custom. In Ogden (State of Utah), the first train to enter the new railway station for the inaugural ceremony was *towed* in by a *mob*, ... of pretty, young ladies from the town."

There she was—in the picture, pulling engine Number 2 into the depot by one of its thirteen ribbons!

Courtesy of Ogden Union Station Museums

* * * *

Friday, November 13, 1925

Fate! she said to herself, looking at the blue dress, once again hanging from the window latch. If not fate, then what?

It was fate I got picked to wash the dress. And it was fate that I wore it and because of it, my handsome Stefano noticed me. It was fate too that the movie star ended up leaving without her laundry, so there was no one to miss the Carolina-blue dress in the bundle returned to the hotel.

A chill draft, sneaking through a gap in the window frame of her shabby dwelling, made the fancy fabric seem like it breathed. Amelia hugged herself and pressed her lips together to contain the smile bursting to flower on her face. She thought it only natural she should wear the blue chiffon dress today, for the second time, to meet Stefano at Union Station.

Dreamily humming "What'll I Do," her eyes drifted to the newspaper clipping she had tacked on the wall several months before, and which continued to read, "Curious American Custom…Ogden Society Girls…" But she couldn't feel lighthearted about it anymore. Lately, it was like something cold slipped into her belly every time she glanced at it.

For months, she had skimmed over her life in Ogden, purposely omitting a great deal in her letters to Stefano. She let him believe she was the Ogden Society Girl he mistook her for when they met.

A man who writes such letters as Stefano can't possibly object to a working American woman, Amelia told herself as she styled her bobbed hair in finger curls. And anyway, it would be best to tell him face-to-face—I can't very well say, "I'm a laundress," in a letter.

Still, the uneasy feeling continued to do circles in her belly. What if he does object?

He won't.

Once again, she left her building the back way, Stefano's face foremost in her mind.

Amelia did an ungainly walk-trot all the way to Union Station. Breathless and cold, she traversed the Grand Lobby and skipped down the stairs into the passenger subway to get to the tracks. She wanted to be under the butterfly canopy waiting for Stefano. Her heart galloped in her chest as the train pulled into the station and she spotted him, leaning out of one of the carriage doors. She took that to mean he was just as eager to see her and began bouncing on the spot, waving with both arms raised.

Stefano laughed and bounded off the train before it even stopped. He scooped her into his arms. "*Cara*," he whispered in her ear and kissed her, then and there.

Amelia melted into the long-awaited embrace.

The opportune moment to tell him the truth of her situation didn't come for over four hours—the most wondrous four hours of Amelia's life! At the end of that time, Stefano guided her back, north of the depot, "Where I first saw you," he told her, dropping to one knee by the empty tracks.

He held up a golden band to her. "Consent to be my wife," he said, looking at her as a man long-lost in the desert might look at a pitcher of cold water. "And I will devote my life to making you happy."

Amelia believed him. She smiled and fell to her knees in front of him. "Yes!" she exclaimed, "I knew how it would be, my Stefano!" she sighed, and all the details she had omitted in her letters tumbled out of her, as Stefano nuzzled and kissed her neck.

Gradually his kissing slowed and then stopped altogether.

Brow furrowed, he stood but didn't offer to help her to her feet. He walked away as if deep in thought. It didn't occur to Amelia to get off her knees—she stared after him, blindsided by the inexplicable reaction, until Stefano turned back to face her.

"You deceived me," he declared, with the finality of a judge's gavel in a courtroom.

Amelia gasped. His eyes were cold on her, full of loathing. "Stefano, please!" she cried, getting unsteadily back on her feet, feeling like her knees might buckle.

He let out a mirthless laugh that froze Amelia to the core.

"A laundress! Passing yourself for a rich woman." She could hear the disgust in his voice, the shame of having been tricked.

"Stefano, I am telling you now," she cried. "I work hard for a living, what is wrong with that?"

He didn't answer. He jumped onto the eastbound track and ran several yards out.

She followed. If she could hold him and kiss him, she could make him understand how trivial this was compared to the love she felt for him. "Listen to me, please!"

Her T-bar shoes weren't managing the gravel between the tracks very well. Amelia stumbled.

Several feet ahead, Stefano stopped and turned to glare at her. "You have been such a waste of my time!" he spat. She watched him pitch the gold ring up the track with all his might. She heard it land.

"Nooooo!" She half crawled, half ran to him. "Please listen to me."

Stefano wrestled her off but held onto her wrists. He shook her roughly. "You will never see me or hear from me again, do you understand?"

"Stefano, please, I love you!"

He shoved her away with an angry growl. "Not ever!"

Amelia looked from Stefano's retreating back to the empty eastbound track. She wanted Stefano's ring; she wanted Stefano. Blinded by tears, she took off up the track, but couldn't space her steps between ties. Her foot gave way with an ominous sound of cracking bones.

The distant whistle of a train reached her ears. *I must get off the track,* she thought. The gravel hurt her skin; she could feel it through the Carolina-blue chiffon.

The hot pain in her ankle felt like an electrical current; it made her whole leg throb. She couldn't see Stefano anymore, but from where she lay panting, the ring glittered a few feet in front of her.

Amelia could feel it in her chest—the clattering of the train and the rattling tracks, as she dragged herself over ties and gravel. Her fingers closed around the gold circle.

She looked up, jubilant. *Now, I must roll off the track!*

All she saw was the monstrous No. 2 on the snout of the locomotive.

Amelia's mouth opened and an infinite, desolate scream escaped.

* * * *

Friday, November 13, 2015

"Did you hear that?" I blurted, grabbing my daughter by the elbow. "Did you see it?"

"See what?" she asked, looking at me alarmed.

My mind racing, I stared at the empty eastbound track and pointed. "There—she was on those tracks, and she had a blue dress on."

I put my hand over my heart—I could feel a horrible, ancient ache there. *Listen to me, please!* My eyes filled with tears and I tried to swallow the lump at the top of my throat.

"Mom?"

"Didn't you hear it—a long drawn-out wail?" I asked again, refusing to believe the experience had been mine alone. "The saddest sound I've ever heard!"

We stood side by side, staring at the deserted track a moment longer; my daughter, probably wondering if I'd lost my mind, and me, trying to shake off the heart-breaking quality of the cry that had rattled me to my bones.

The distant whistle of the approaching Front Runner train began to dispel the trance, but before it let me go, I turned to my daughter, gripped by a sudden conviction. A deep-rooted acknowledgement burst from me: "That bastard broke my heart!"

Locals and visitors to Union Station, at the west end of Historic 25th Street in Ogden, claim to have heard an anguished scream uttered by a lady dressed in blue—she is on the railroad tracks.

The well-known legend tells the story of a jilted woman who could not fathom living with a broken heart, but the tale whispered to me suggests a tragic misunderstanding.

* * * *

Factual tidbit about *Carolina Blue*:

Below is a thumbnail of the original image taken during the Ogden Depot Opening in 1924.

A full-color reproduction of it was featured on the front page of *La Domenica del Corriere*'s January 25, 1925 issue, with this legend: "Curious American Custom"

Both images, including the one on page 166, are courtesy of Ogden Union Station Museums, and they were my inspiration when I set out to figure out the identity of the Lady in Blue.

A WORD FROM
EDITORIAL REVIEWERS AND BETA READERS:

"…these deliciously gruesome stories are very carefully crafted. They begin in such a way that the reader is immediately drawn in, curiosity is aroused, disbelief is suspended, and the book cannot be set down, till the story is done…" –Sherry Hogg, author of *Child of Mine* and select *Tales from Two-Bit Street and Beyond*

"I felt like I was sitting around a campfire, hanging out with a group of friends, trying to scare one another."—Tiffany Rankin

"Each town, village, and hamlet has their own ghost stories, passed down from parent to child throughout generations. Some are used to keep wayward children in line, while others are used to warn youth about the perils of challenging evil, or the pitfalls of unrequited love. These *Seven Ghostly Spins* are such tales… read them to your wee ones, just remember to leave a light on." –Deborah Mitton, author of the series *A Murder of Crows*

"It's amazing how every time I read this author's work I am taken directly into the worlds she creates… sometimes I look up from the book and am surprised to be in my room or office reading and not looking through an iron gate, staring at a headstone, walking through an old brothel or camping in the desert. A suspenseful page turner where the endings reminded me of one my favorite 80's shows, the Hitchhiker…I would always get chills and wonder…hmmm" –Paul Wold

"*Seven Ghostly Spins*: A Brush with the Supernatural, by Patricia Bossano and Kelsey E. Gerard lives up to its name and provides short but enjoyable stories that are mysterious and creepy, but not over the top horror-filled… Each of the seven stories is unique and memorable…" –Literary Titan

"What an emotional roller coaster the stories were… Never stop writing!" –Outi Gomez

"Thrilling ghost stories that remind me of the Twilight Zone series. Kelsey E. Gerard's writing style as a debut author is very good and it fits with Bossano's established voice. *Seven Ghostly Spins* is a fun and easy read that is hard to put down. The stories are well written, and the authors have a wonderful imagination. I look forward to reading their next book."
–Kirk Raeber, author of *Forgotten Letters*

ABOUT THE AUTHORS

PATRICIA BOSSANO
Award-winning author of the philosophical fantasy novels,
Faery Sight, *Cradle Gift*, *Nahia*, and other supernatural tales.
She lives in California with her family.
www.patriciabossano.com

Featured author: *She Caught A Ride*
KELSEY E. GERARD
Fiction writer, distinguished contributor to her alma mater's *Metaphor*
Undergraduate Literary Journal, and aspiring professional scribbler.
Currently residing in Northern Utah.

CPSIA information can be obtained
at www.ICGtesting.com
Printed in the USA
LVHW030422170119
604234LV00002B/392